FIRST TIME IN PAPERBACK!

INCIDENT AT SUN MOUNTAIN

The Comstock Lode—men went mad with greed at even the mere mention of the incredible silver strike. But the times were troubled, with Yankees and Rebels choosing sides. The Civil War was drawing near, and the side with more wealth was bound to win the bloody conflict. From Nevada boomtowns to the Barbary Coast, trouble was brewing between Northern loyalists and Confederate insurgents. If not for valiant men like Ken English, the unlimited riches of the Comstock Lode might fall prey to Southern turncoats—and the glorious United States might perish forever....

TODHUNTER BALLARD

Todhunter Ballard is renowned for his bold sagas of the pioneers who tamed the West. The author of more than fifty novels, he is the winner of the Spur Award for Best Historical Novel.

Other *Leisure Books* by Todhunter Ballard:
GOLD IN CALIFORNIA!
THE CALIFORNIAN

TODHUNTER BALLARD

Incident At Sun Mountain

LEISURE BOOKS NEW YORK CITY

A LEISURE BOOK®

March 1996

Published by special arrangement with Golden West Literary Agency.

Dorchester Publishing Co., Inc.
276 Fifth Avenue
New York, NY 10001

Printed in the United States of America.

Incident At Sun Mountain

Author's Note

Much has been written about Virginia City and the amazing Comstock Lode. The silver which was mined from the heart of Sun Mountain was the foundation for a hundred fortunes; it built San Francisco and played a heavy share in developing the west coast states.

But its political and economic effect was even greater than the impact which it had on Western history. Nevada was admitted as a state for the sole purpose of ratifying the amendment freeing the slaves. At the time, Nevada consisted of nothing more than a few scattered mining camps and the principal population was centered around Sun Mountain.

The Southern leaders were well aware of the mountain's importance, just as they had been aware of the Pacific coast importance from the time of the first discovery of gold. The Golden Circle, which had its conception in a filibustering scheme that would have blanketed the whole central American section with the Southern States in a slaveholding empire, has been curiously neglected by history.

It was in the first place a secret organization, and most of the Copperhead movements which caused the Northern Government trouble during the Civil War drew their beginnings from the Circle.

It was particularly powerful all along the west coast since many of the settlers had migrated from the South, but there is strong evidence to show that its western center during the first months of the war was in Nevada and that Judge Terry was its head.

At that time the Southerners might well have seized the Lode and the whole of the west coast. History shows that for a matter of five or six weeks they were in actual control of Sun Mountain. That Judge Terry chose to throw away this advantage, that he should suddenly desert Nevada and ride south, just at the moment when the western country was about to fall into his lap, is one of the challenging mysteries which any reader will find in studying the period.

I am indebted to a number of people for their interest, kindness and assistance. To the staffs of the Pasadena, Los Angeles, Huntington and the Bancroft Libraries, to the Nevada State Library, to a private collector who kindly made available his almost complete file of the *Territorial Enterprise.* And finally to Miss Gillis and Miss Wenzell of the California State Library at Sacramento who, with their staffs, gave unstintingly of their time and help during the year which I spent studying the material in the California Room.

TODHUNTER BALLARD

Chapter One

Sunset caught the hurrying stage seven hours out of Placerville, still climbing steadily the writhing road which breasted the west slope of the Sierras.

The long shadows lengthened as the sun dropped behind the granite upthrust of the snowy crest and the downdraft brought the icy wind sweeping along the twisting trail to strike fully against Ken English.

He sat on the exposed seat beside the driver and had nothing to break the force of the wind save his heavy blanket coat. He shivered, turning up the collar, and stared at the endless line of lumbering freight wagons. These wagons moved in a continuing stream, crawling team to tail-board up the rugged grade, down the eastern slope, across the short desert and so into the new Washoe mining district.

A tall man, English rode loosely against the sway of the careening stage. Beside him the cursing driver tooled the big Concord expertly between the line of the slow-moving wagons and the rim of the shelflike road.

At times they were so near the edge that English could look almost straight down through the big pines to the rushing river a thousand feet below them.

The narrow canyon vibrated with tumult, the shouts of the weary teamsters, the bells on the high-bowed mule yokes, the keening grind of the iron tires, and always the cloud of sound set up by the dried-out, chattering body of the stage.

Darkness rose over them before they swept around a high turn, forced a hole in the slow wagon line, and pulled into the stage station.

Under the trees the crowded station yard was already lighted by flaring pine knots. Hostlers ran forward. Hap Small, the driver, fastened his lines and leaned down to shout through the glassless side window, "Strawberry, Strawberry! Thirty minutes for grub!"

He turned then, his square-cut red beard bobbing as he gave English his small boy's grin. "You don't scare worth a damn, friend. Maybe I'm losing my touch. They usually turn green when they ride with me."

He waited for no answer, but dropping down over the wheel, he stalked away toward the station, not once looking back.

English chuckled, and followed the driver to the ground. As he stretched his legs, his blue-gray eyes swept the yard, estimating the throng with a quick, studying calculation.

The yard had been tramped clear of snow and here and there campfires burned where weary travelers had spread their blankets and slept, unmindful of the hubbub of the constant movement around them.

Off to the right, tethered teams had been pulled out for rest. Beyond them, their drivers labored at the outdoor forge which blazed hotly for the use of all.

In the center squatted the main station building, some forty feet in length. Built of unpeeled logs, its glazeless windows squares of naked light, it promised all the welcome of a hostile blockhouse.

English ignored the other passengers descending stiffly behind him, pushed across the yard to the open door, and fought his way inside.

There he was halted. The long low room was jammed. There were simply more people within the rough walls than could find sufficient space to move.

Across the heads of the mob English had a look at the big tables, but judged that it would be hopeless to reach them within his allotted time.

Turning, he forged back through the door, breasting the new arrivals, using his elbows freely, deaf to the muttered curses until he again gained the comparative freedom of the open.

He paused, filling his lungs with air.

The door of the motionless stage opened and the girl appeared on the step, hesitating, undecided, looking out across the yard to the log building.

She was facing English and in the sputtering light from the flaring torches she made a picture which was complete and satisfying and beautiful.

English remained motionless, his eyes narrowing with attention as he photographed her beauty on his memory.

Abruptly she turned, disappearing back into the gloomy shelter of the stage, letting the heavy door swing shut behind her.

English released his held breath in a long, almost toneless whistle. He had forgotten she was on the coach, and the long night's ride ahead would be grueling enough without an empty stomach. He glanced back into the crowded room, then turned sharply right and circled the log building.

He walked with the short choppy stride of a man who is more used to riding, his boots crackling the thin crust of frozen ground as he passed the pole corrals and the stacks of mountain hay.

The back door was of heavy planking. It failed to give when he tried it and he beat upon it with his fist. He got no answer and drawing his Navy revolver he used its heavy butt.

Still there was no response. English retreated a step and slammed his heavy boot sole against the center of the door. It groaned, held, and he tried again.

He was rewarded. A bar was withdrawn. The door swung inward to expose the heavy bearded face of Al Berry. The station keeper held a shotgun in his hamlike hands, and his eyes gleamed like blue slots in the red puffiness of his angry face.

"Get away from this door." He shoved the gun barrels at English's chest.

Ken still held his Navy by its heavy barrel. He spoke softly. "There's a lady on the stage. We've only thirty minutes to eat."

Berry grunted. Arrogant, he ruled the station with the unreasonablness of a petty dictator. "She'll take her chances with the rest," he grumbled. "We play no favorites, and if she's traveling to Washoe, the chances are she ain't no lady."

He started to chuckle at his coarse humor, showing discolored teeth through the uneven part of his beard, but the sound cut short as English flipped the heavy revolver, caught its smooth stock.

"I'll take two plates," his tone was even, "and coffee, or would you rather see if you can pull that scattergun faster than I can work this trigger?"

Berry hesitated, glaring at the clean-shaven face before him. He was a bully, used to lording it over stranded travelers, but there was something in the even set of this stranger's jaw, in the steady blue-gray eyes which warned him that English was not bluffing.

Grumbling, he leaned his gun against the door jamb and turning to the big stove filled two tin plates with beans, boiled potatoes, and a hunk of sour bread.

The coffee which he slopped into the cups was jet-black, bitter. He sweetened it with a dash of molasses.

"Two dollars each."

Still holding the Colt, English fished out four silver slugs with his free hand and tossed them to the middle of the kitchen floor.

He indicated that the plates be placed on the step beside the full cups, but not until the door had slammed and he heard the heavy bar dropped in place did he thrust the gun back under his belt and pick up the food.

Holding the loaded plates high, he turned across the crowded yard toward the motionless stage and had almost reached it when the mob swayed against him, giving way for a dozen well-mounted men who swept in from the road and heedless of the panic they caused drove through the throng toward the corrals.

A miner, thrust back against English in the press, cursed angrily. "Terry's men. Damn secesh! They think they own Washoe. They think they own the world."

English stood perfectly still, staring after the riders, then he turned and plodded to the coach and spoke through the open window.

"I brought you something to eat, ma'am. We've a long night's ride ahead of us."

The girl had been staring out of the far window at the busy road. She turned at the sound of his voice, her startled brown eyes examining him with uneasy attention.

"I'm harmless," he said. "The name is English, Ken English, and I've never been known to bite anyone."

He did not smile, but one corner of his tight-lipped mouth lifted without disturbing the other and his eyes crinkled at the corners.

She laughed with nervous lightness. "I'm sure you can't be that harmless, but I'm so starved I'd accept food from the devil himself." She leaned forward to take the plate and coffee cup from his upstretched hand. "I'd given up hope. The yard was crowded and it looked worse inside."

"It was," said English, with a slight smile. "But I knew a man . . ."

"You, you're with the stage company?"

"No, ma'am. I saw you get aboard at Placerville, and I saw you start out for food a while ago, then change your mind." He started to turn away, but she stopped him diffidently.

"Couldn't you eat more comfortably in here?"

"Why, yes." He was surprised by the invitation, but swung up, taking the facing seat and resting his plate on his knee. "It's nice of you to ask me."

"I could hardly do less, Mr. English, after you provided the food." She noted his studying eyes and lowered her own.

They ate in silence, she with not too much relish, while English cleaned his plate with the dogged determination of a man who had known hunger.

She watched him finish the last dregs of bitter coffee. He saw her look of distaste and grinned. "It isn't the best in the world," he told here, "but it fills you. Sometimes that can be important. It's something you learn on the trail. Never pass water without drinking, never miss a meal until you have to."

She nodded silently, letting him take her half-empty plate which he carried to a nearby tree and placed on the ground.

As he came back to the stage the hostlers appeared, leading the fresh horses.

The girl spoke ruefully. "I wonder if I could ask one more favor. The man who has the seat beside me is a whiskey drummer who has been sampling his own wares."

Without a word English climbed back into the stage and took the seat at her side, surprised at the sense of warm pleasure her request gave him.

"I'm Mary Frances Everett," she said. "My father has stores in San Francisco and Sacramento, and he's opening one at Carson. He's talking about Gold Hill and Virginia."

She watched his face as if expecting him to recognize the name, but his eyes showed only polite interest.

"Father will never forgive me for making this trip alone," she added.

"It isn't the safest thing for a woman to do."

"You men." She sounded half angry. "No one ever believes a girl can take care of herself. I can shoot as well as a man, and I rode before I was ten." Her mood changed. "I should have been a man. I'd have loved being a miner, or a gambler, or both."

"Would you? I hardly believe so."

She looked at him directly. There was nothing of the coquette about her. "Why wouldn't I? Are you a miner, Mr. English, or perhaps a gambler? I hope you are. I'd love to shock Father, telling him that the one gentleman I met on the trip turned out to be a card sharp."

He guessed that she was making fun of him and did not care. There was an impish quality about her which only made her more attractive.

"Sorry to disappoint you," his mock gravity matched her own, "but I have terrible luck with cards. Let's say that I'm a traveler, a man out to seek his fortune."

The girl's voice deepened. "You're very lucky. You can come to Washoe, or go to the northern mines, or where you choose. A girl is held by silly conventions, she must observe the niceties. She's never free. She has to guard her actions or cease to be a respectable female. Do I sound crazy? My father says I am. He's threatened to lock me up more than once."

English thought, She's still making fun of me. She probably makes fun of her father and he doesn't suspect. At least she doesn't take life too seriously.

His thoughts were interrupted by the returning passengers, sulky and supperless. Not one of them had managed to reach the tables.

The whiskey drummer was a beefy man, fleshy and of great self-importance. He stared angrily at English, opening his loose mouth to demand his seat, but at English's cold, questioning smile he turned away muttering and climbed heavily to the top of the coach.

Hap Small appeared, walking leisurely as if he knew that without him the world would cease to move. He adjusted his gauntlets, found English beside the girl, gave him a studying smile, climbed to his place and freed the lines. Then his bull-like cry split the night.

"Away, away for Washoe!"

The hostlers jumped clear, the team lurched forward into its collars. Fresh and full of run, the horses took the lumbering stage out of the yard at a full gallop.

Chapter Two

Towering eight thousand feet into the thin air, Sun Mountain was the highest peak in the Washoe range. A ragged spur of the Sierras, it thrust out into the flat desert, frowning above the green valley of the Carson which flowed along its eastern base.

Virginia City, largest of the Comstock towns, nestled in a wide shelving canyon more than halfway to the summit. Below and over the eastern divide lay Gold Hill and Silver City, and at the foot of the mountain wound the emigrant trail along which half a hundred settlements had sprung into being, fed by the new strike.

Standing at the window of his room in the International Hotel, Ken English stared down at the tangle of crooked streets which twisted between the rows of tent buildings and straggling shacks.

He had seen other mining camps. Six years on the frontier had accustomed him to the surging excitement which gripped men in their search for wealth, but never before had he witnessed such frenzy as he saw on these crowded paths.

California towns were half deserted. Prosperous mines had shut down while their owners joined the new rush. Men who had built respected places for themselves in law and business and medicine closed their offices in the Golden State and came over the mountains to Washoe. It was a surging tidal wave, sucked on by the glowing prospects of the new camp.

Already business houses flanked the full length of the three main streets and the whole outcropping of the reef which held the silver riches locked in its matrix was so studded with claims, shaft houses, and working pits that the openings overlapped while the underground drifts and tunnels interlocked, and the miners battled each other as well as the stubborn earth to work out the rich ore.

It was a mêlée of confusion, blanketed by a torrent of noise, shrilling steam whistles, deafening thunder from the tireless stamps, and always the high, shrill, wordless chorus of the crowding teamsters.

The wooden sidewalks were hidden from English's gaze by the tide of restless men, gamblers, prospectors, speculators, flowing in and out of the saloons, the gambling halls, the brokerage offices, drinking, carousing, trading in claims, in mines and mining feet, buying and selling thousands upon thousands more shares than actually existed on the whole lode.

Each was a millionaire in his own mind, each was certain that fortune had turned his way. They had proof, they could see with their own eyes the heaped ore wagons, the bullion bars, stacked for shipment in the express office. The very air was thick with blue dust, dust that powdered the shabby structures, the rutted streets, the crowd, even the food they ate with a thin yet actual layer of raw silver.

A man needed but to brush his hair to see the stuff. He breathed it, smelled it, lived with it . . . silver, Washoe silver! No wonder the whole western world seemed to have gone mad.

But English, staring down at the confusion below him, knew a feeling of deep depression. While the frenzied crowd struggled for riches, events were framing outside the narrow confines of this canyon, events which would shape the future history of the nation.

As if in answer to his thought someone knocked on the door, and turning away from the window he called, "It isn't locked."

Tom Burke stepped in. English had never met

Burke, but the man had been so thoroughly described that there was no possibility of error. The ex-New Yorker was as tall as English, heavier, but not yet fat. His blue eyes were steady and he carried himself with an air of proud disdain which in itself was an unspoken dare to his many enemies.

He stopped just inside the door, his eyes turning frosty as he realized that he was in the presence of a stranger.

"They told me downstairs that a friend was waiting for me in this room."

"Shut the door," said English.

The chief engineer of the Volunteer Fire Department hesitated, not from fear, but the last year had taught Tom Burke the elements of caution.

Despite the seeming unmindfulness of the street crowds, politics were very real to the citizens of Sun Mountain. Even in their blind struggle for quick wealth, they found themselves split sharply into angry groups and for months the leaders on both sides had carried on a grim, beneath-the-surface struggle for power.

Tom Burke shut the door quietly, never taking his sharp eyes from English's face. He saw a man matured beyond his years, a squarish face turned brown by wind and weather, a tight, thoughtful mouth, mobile yet indicating strength.

Burke had learned early to judge men and he judged this one quickly, noting the dragoon straightness of the back, the easy, on-balance movement of the tall body.

"You seem to know my name?"

"Mine's English," Ken told him. "The name will mean nothing. This will." He unbuttoned the front of his rough shirt and drew out a flat packet which he handed silently to his visitor.

Burke accepted the packet, but made no effort to break the seals. "Now who would be sending me a letter by you?"

"You wrote Senator Seward, I believe."

The tightening of the muscles at the corner of his eyes was Burke's only indication of surprise. He studied English for a long moment before he slit the cover and read the short message with the deliberateness of one who knew far more about engines than he did letters.

When he had finished he regarded English reflectively. "I ask for a decisive military force," his tone was bitter, "and they send one man. Are there nothing but fools in the East? Can't they realize what is happening out here, Lieutenant?"

English kept his temper. "That's why I came, to make a careful study and report . . ."

"Report, report . . ." Burke's patience, never his strong quality, gave way and he exploded. "In hell's name what good are reports? I wrote the Senator fully. Does Seward take me for a liar? I warned him that unless there was action at once Washoe would be lost to the Union, yes, and California too. No one will believe how strong the secessionists are here . . ."

He broke off helplessly, staring above English's head as if his blue eyes could already see the rising ranks of rebels marching triumphantly across his beloved mountain, then controlling his feelings with a visible effort he went on in a quieter tone.

"There's always been strong Southern sentiment in California. For years there's been talk of forming a western republic, taking in the whole coast, part of Mexico, and Texas. That idea still has strong support."

English nodded. "I read your letter to the Senator, but as he said, you offered little proof and . . ."

"Proof, when a man's house is burning does he demand proof? In God's name, what do they want me to tell them?"

English had been warned of Burke's temper and had schooled himself for this meeting. He said, evenly, "Senator Seward feels that at this time, with tempers strained to the breaking point, we should move carefully and antagonize no one while the chance to preserve the Union remains."

Burke stared at him. "I've been a soldier," he

said, slowly. "I realize that you consider yourself under orders, but . . ."

"I'm no longer in the army," English told him gravely. "I came here as the Senator's personal representative to see . . ."

"Then tell Seward this. Tell him the North has tried to appease the South for years, and that every effort, every compromise has been taken as a sign of weakness.

"Tell him that Judge Terry has bragged in public that he holds a commission signed by Jeff Davis, that when war comes, Terry intends to seize the Sun Mountain mines, in the name of the South. Tell Seward that Terry has guns, the only military arms on the Comstock, that he has organized well-drilled companies, that he has built stone forts, one of which you can see from that window, and that they mean to finance the Southern armies with Washoe silver. This is not suspicion on my part, this is a fact."

English was impressed by Burke's vehemence. "Have you relayed this information to the military authorities at San Francisco?"

"The military authorities at San Francisco!" Burke gave him a pitying look. "Listen, Lieutenant. General Johnston knows more about Terry's plans than I do. They are both Texans. Johnston has made no secret of where his sympathy lies. If the South secedes, Johnston means to resign. The West is deserted, Lieutenant. We are in the hands of our enemies. It would serve these new Republicans right if we joined the rebels. That's why I wrote Seward. I don't know this Lincoln, but I know Seward. For years he has led the fight against slavery. I expected him to be nominated."

English smiled slightly. Seward himself had expected the nomination.

Burke ignored the smile. "Everyone says that Seward will be in the new Cabinet. Certainly he's the most experienced man in the party. He'll probably run the show."

English did not answer. Burke was right. Seward was the most widely known man in the new party, certainly more prominent than the country lawyer who had been elected President, and who even then was waiting to be inaugurated.

And Seward did expect to be in the Cabinet. Already he was acting as if he were Secretary of State. His instructions to English had been simple.

"I'm sending you because you've seen service on the frontier and understand its people. I want no sudden spark to ignite the powder keg. I still feel certain that once we take office we can resolve our quarrels with our southern neighbors. But men like Burke frighten me. I know he's entirely loyal, but I fear misguided and inclined to overrate the grumblings of his fellow miners.

"You are on your own. I have no authority to

send you until after Lincoln is inaugurated, but events will not wait. Quiet Burke, watch these Southern agitators, but do nothing which might worsen the situation, and let no one save Burke know that you come from me."

Burke had been watching him. "You don't take me very seriously." He was bitter. "All right, go out and see for yourself, walk into Terry's forts, join his crowd, listen to their brags, see their arms, but don't admit that you know me.

"Terry has marked my fire companies as the only organization on the whole mountain that stands in his way. There would be joy at the next meeting of the Golden Circle if they could report my death."

English started. "The Golden Circle, out here? You mean there are filibusterers on the Comstock?"

"Ask Terry." Burke was still bitter. "They might take you in as a member. Certainly you and Seward are helping them by your indifference, whether you know it or not." He backed up and grasped the knob angrily. The next moment he vanished into the hall, slamming the door behind him.

Chapter Three

The Silver Lode Saloon was no different from a dozen of its fellows. A long room, its flooring of rough planks, its roof still canvas, it yet made some pretensions to the grandeur it would achieve in later years.

Shortly after dark Ken English turned into its wide door, finding the yellow lamp glow welcome after the growing murkiness of the street.

The wind whistling over the divide was chill, bearing the sharp, penetrating cold of the spring snows. All afternoon he had tramped the streets, listening to the chance conversations of the crowd, forming his own picture of the town.

In his first report to Seward, written to catch the "pony" before the express rider swept down the long trail for the East, he had repeated

Burke's words, and added the fears which had been growing steadily within him during the day.

"Nothing I can write," he began, "will give you a true conception of this place. The mountain has to be seen to be understood, and the men here are a race apart. Hardened by the gold camps, they are facing new problems here and solving them daily.

"The ore, complex by California standards, is unbelievably rich, and some prophesy that the veins will widen to a hundred feet as the mines deepen. Even if they're wrong, it is probably the greatest natural storehouse of wealth the world will ever see. The veins are twenty to forty feet wide, running close to half pure silver with good values in gold.

"Think then what this treasure can mean if we are forced to fight the South, which brings up the point of this report. I talked to Burke, and then I went out to see for myself. At times I could have closed my eyes and from the conversation around me imagined myself in Montgomery or Charleston. The sentiment against the North could not be more outspoken in any southern town than it is here.

"And it is not all talk. Judge Terry, who killed Senator Broderick in that unfortunate duel, is the acknowledged leader of the separation movement. He has built three forts upon the lode which are garrisoned by armed men, and it is rumored that he heads the local council of the Knights of the Golden Circle, that filibustering organization which has its headquarters in Cuba where Lopez plans to form an empire, taking in the Caribbean states and welding them into a vast slaveholding power.

"The situation is further complicated by the distrust with which the local unionist leaders view General Johnston. I do not accuse the general of disloyalty, but he is a Texan, as is Terry.

"May I respectfully ask that you show this to Mr. Lincoln and suggest that at this time the military establishment charged with safeguarding the nation's interests on the Pacific should be in the hands of a man whose loyalty is above question."

When he had finished, English reread the letter before carrying it to the express office. Ever since his conversation with Burke the sense of his responsibility had been weighing heavily upon him. One mistake, and this whole section might well secede. What right had he, a private citizen, sent here as Seward's personal representative, to take any action?

But even with the pony express the mountain was remote from the eastern seaboard, and it would take days before he could receive instructions.

And he was incapable of standing by idly and watching Washoe stolen by the Southerners. In

New York Seward's ideas of appeasement had sounded wise, but here in the shadow of Terry's forts he knew instinctively that the time of appeasement was past.

The bartender served him and he was lifting the glass from the bar, which had been built from an old sluice box, when the swinging doors slammed open with a force that was greater than the howling wind and English turned to see a heavy-set man whose round brutal face was framed by long red side whiskers. The whiskers were odd enough, but their owner had increased the effect by tying them under his chin.

He paused just inside the door, staring around the room with red-rimmed eyes, reptilelike in their fixed intensity, then said in a high, carrying voice which washed out other sound, "I'm a chief. I'm the biggest chief in Washoe."

He got no answer and advanced to the bar, a kind of one-man parade as the drinkers fell back out of his path.

He came against the rough counter four feet from English and gestured at the bartender with a big hand. "Set 'em up! I'm Sam Brown. I ain't killed a man all day. I've got to have me a dead man for supper."

There was a mirror behind the shelf which served as a back bar and in its depths English watched the man, noting the effect his arrival had had on the crowd.

It was silent, apprehensive. Men who had been drinking quietly a moment before were drifting toward the far corners, trying to make the movement as unobtrusive as possible, fearing that somehow they might attract the chief's unfavorable attention.

One had not moved, a slight boy who held his place beyond Brown, ignoring the new arrival completely as if buried in his own thoughts.

English had his back half turned to Brown, his big body leaning forward, his weight balanced by his left elbow. He too gave no sign that he saw Brown although he kept watching the mirror.

The bartender, red-faced and nervous, moved to face Brown, shoving a square bottle and glass before the bad man, then retreating to the far end where he managed to appear busy with his polishing cloth.

Brown's eyes were sardonic as they watched him, then they swung slowly as their owner appraised English, noting the Navy protruding from Ken's waistband, the haft of the knife which showed above the top of Ken's boot.

In some respect Sam Brown was careful. In all his killings, both in Plumas County and in Washoe, he chose friendless men, or unimportant men whose appearance promised little threat to his own safety.

After his long look, he picked up the square

bottle, filling his glass twice for two quick drinks, then wiped his lips with the back of a broad, none too clean hand and said to no one in particular, "We're taking over the lode." He spat, the spittle making its small ugliness beside the glass. "All of you had better run, I'm telling you. The Golden Circle will clear this camp of sniveling Yankees."

"You talk too much." It was the boy beyond Brown.

Sam Brown turned slowly as if he could not believe that anyone would dare correct him. "You meaning me?" His big hand dropped to cover the handle of his knife. "Dammit, I'll have your ears."

"I said you talk too much." The boy had not raised his voice. It was low, rich with soft southern overtones. "Judge Terry should hang you by the thumbs to teach you manners."

Brown concentrated on the boy, weighing him, probing him, and decided that he was of no great importance.

"Damn Terry," he said. "And damn you, Vance Youngman. You're nobody. You're scum." He pulled the long knife clear of its protecting sheath. Its broad sixteen-inch blade, honed to a razor's edge, glittered in the yellow lamplight.

And then Brown began to stalk his victim, his big body bending forward like a tautly depressed spring.

Vance Youngman closed his small hand around the neck of the whiskey bottle and took a step away from the bar. Two spots of bright color burned in his sensitive face, and his eyes which had been carefree and unmindful were suddenly deep with anger, laced with fear.

"You drunken fool. Put up that knife. Terry will . . ."

"Terry will what . . . ?" Sam Brown's heavy tones mocked the boy. "You think you're important, Mr. Youngman. Let me ask you this. How many fights have you won? How many men have you killed? Don't fool yourself. Terry needs fighters." He chuckled. "Terry will thank me for putting a couple of inches of steel in your windpipe."

He took another step.

English turned his body without moving his feet. He expected half the men in the room to come to the boy's aid, for it was obvious that Youngman was not armed. But no one moved as the killer took a third step.

Brown was in no hurry, a huge, hairy brute, prolonging the suspense purposely as if he savored each lingering moment of the boy's growing panic.

"First I'll shave your ears."

Youngman stood clutching the whiskey bottle, afraid, yet obviously too proud to run.

"Hold it," said English. The last thing he

wanted was to attract attention to himself in a barroom fight, but he could not stand by and see the boy butchered.

Brown stopped. He stood motionless, the knife grasped in his thick palm, point thrust forward. He was too old a hand to swing about, leaving Youngman at his rear, until he had appraised this new danger.

His eyes went to the mirror above the back bar and he gave English's reflection a long, studying look, deciding that Ken was far more dangerous than Vance Youngman.

He turned slowly then, stepping backward toward the center of the room. Thus the three of them formed the points of a shallow triangle, and Brown had his back to neither.

His eyes, prominent and bloodshot from his drinking, watched English, not liking what they saw. Here was no boy, ripe for slaughter, but a man, standing taller than he did, watchful, waiting.

"I'm Sam Brown," the bad man announced in his grumbling voice. "I'm the Chief of the Comstock. When I howl, the other chiefs run and hide. Maybe you never heard of me, stranger."

"Maybe I never did." English's tone was larded with disinterest. He could not have stung Brown's vanity more if he had cursed the chief in a dozen languages. Sam Brown's ego fed on the panicky fear of other men. He welcomed it more than praise, needed it more than food.

Already he knew that he must kill English, or the story that Sam Brown had been faced down would be all over the lode before morning.

Yet he feared the coming fight and he uttered words which his lips detested. "This quarrel isn't yours." he said. "Move out." He jerked his bushy head toward the side door.

English stared at him, then at Youngman. The boy stood beside the bar, still clutching his whiskey bottle, caught by surprise at the quick shift of events. Ken nodded. "Sure, I'll go and take him with me."

Brown cursed and charged without warning, trying by his leaping bound to pin English against the bar, his knife held forward like the point of a leveled spear.

The move was so rapid that Ken had no chance to pull his own knife, no opportunity to free his gun. He held a glass of whiskey in his hand and he threw it, glass and all, directly into the charging man's bearded face.

The glass struck the high bridge of Brown's nose, spraying the fiery liquid in a blinding stream which peppered his eyes.

English moved sidewise with the agility of a trained boxer and Brown came heavily against the bar at the exact spot where Ken had stood.

The point of his outthrust knife buried itself in the rough wood so deeply that he had to pull twice to free the blade, then he whirled by instinct, seeking his opponent with a wide sweep of his left arm.

English made no effort to avoid the questing hand. Instead he seized it, just above the wrist, and swung Brown around as if the big man had been standing on a pivot, then as the chief turned he chopped at the man's red neck with a rabbit punch that had behind it the full strength of his powerful shoulders.

This was no sparring contest. He well knew that he was fighting for his life, and he used every barroom trick.

The blow did not put Brown down, but it staggered him and he fought for a moment, trying to regain his balance. English kicked his feet from under him.

Brown went down then, the knife spinning from his grasp as he grabbed for support which was not there, but in the last instant before he fell his clawing fingers caught in the edge of English's rough shirt, and he dragged Ken to the floor with him.

As Ken fell he tried to free the man's grasp, twisting his body away from Brown, and so crashed against the bar, cracking his head sharply on the metal foot rail.

He lay for a moment partly stunned, sensing that Brown had rolled over and was trying to gouge his eyes with heavy fingers. He kicked out, his boot catching Brown's stomach. The man grunted, rolling away to come up on his hands and knees.

He crawled off and for an instant English did not sense what he was about, then he realized that Brown was after his fallen knife.

He would have had it. His groping fingers touched the handle, but as he started to pull it toward him Vance Youngman leaped in, kicking it from his grasp.

Brown cursed the boy in a hot, half-strangled voice and struggled to his feet, even as English dragged himself erect with the aid of the bar.

For an instant they stood glaring at each other like two enraged bears, then they closed, without science, standing toe to toe, slugging with all the power of their big bodies, taking punishment and giving it in a desperate madness of which reason had no part.

Brown was the bigger, the heavier, but he was softer and he lacked the reserve staying power of the younger man.

English drove his blows at the massive jaw, but the heavy whiskers, tied beneath the chin, offered a protective cushion which robbed the punches of their explosive force.

He shifted his attack, battering at Brown's short ribs with close, hooking blows. He heard the man grunt, saw by the flicker of the bloodshot eyes that the chief was hurt, and redoubled his efforts, unmindful of the punishment he took around the head.

Brown closed in, trying to stop the blows. He used his superior weight to crowd English, getting his arms around Ken's body, tying him up and then holding him close in a bone-crushing embrace.

The rough whiskers of his cheek cut into English's skin and the man's foul breath almost choked him. He had one paralyzing moment of stark fear, knowing that there would be no reprieves, that Brown was a butcher, a killer with no understanding of the word mercy, and then his brain was functioning again, and since he could not break the smothering grasp he allowed his body to bend with it until he thought that his spinal column must snap.

In sheer desperation he hurled himself backward, taking Brown to the floor with him and so breaking the man's hold.

But he fell underneath, and Brown's body knocked the last remaining air from his tortured lungs. As he lay gasping he realized dimly that instead of throttling him Brown was reaching downward toward the knife in English's boot.

Somewhere Ken found the strength to roll. Throwing the man's heavy body aside he came up to his hands and knees and again used the bar as a ladder to drag himself up.

Behind him Brown was also rising, and Ken,

clinging to the bar with both hands, lashed out in a backward kick, his heavy boot taking the rising man directly in the face.

Brown sat down and as Ken turned the man stared up at him half stupidly. But he was not through. He tried to come off the floor, getting almost to his feet before English charged.

They went down together, both spent. Brown's big hands came up, trying to lock themselves about Ken's throat. English tried to break the grip, failed, and seizing the man's heavy hair he beat Brown's head upon the rough planks of the dirty floor.

The pressure stayed at his gasping throat. He beat harder. He never remembered clearly afterward when Brown's fingers fell away.

Out of nowhere came a number of hands, dragging at his shoulders, lifting him from Brown's limp body. He started to struggle, then stopped as it was borne in upon his shadowed consciousness that the fight was over. Men were shouting. Men were trying to shake his hand, and above the chorus of their voices he heard Youngman yelling, "Give him air. Give him a drink. Let him get his breath. He licked Sam Brown. He's the new Chief of Washoe."

Chapter Four

Even with the salt of fatigue filling his mouth, Ken English knew that he had to get away from the saloon. He waved off the proffered drinks and turning, half blindly felt his way toward the side door. Not until he was on the windy street did he realize that Vance Youngman had followed him.

"That was a fight," the boy said. "You saved my life. I wasn't armed."

The sharp, chill wind was clearing English's battered brain. He felt his taut muscles relaxing and knew that in a few minutes he would be all right. But at the moment he was lackadaisical and uncaring. He wished vaguely that the boy would go away, would leave him alone.

But Youngman was as eager as a friendly pup.

He followed English into the hotel, across the crowded lobby and up the stairs to Ken's room. Once there he settled on one corner of the bed while English stripped off his shirt and with water from the gaudy pitcher laved the grime and blood from his swollen face.

When that was done English examined the damage in the mirror and heard the boy say, "You marked him more than he marked you. This is a great day for Washoe. No one's ever dared to stand against Brown before. He's killed sixteen men in the last year."

English lowered the towel and turned slowly to look at Youngman with unbelieving eyes. "Killed sixteen? That's impossible. Where the hell are the authorities?"

"There is no law on the Comstock," the boy told him. "You must be new here."

"I got in this morning." English had put aside the towel and was searching his duffle for a clean shirt.

"That explains why you were so ready to tackle Sam Brown . . ." The boy broke off, flushing. "That's a fine thing for me to say, and after you saved my life. If I'd had a gun I'd have shot the fool."

English glanced at him. "I'd heard that everyone went armed in Washoe."

Youngman's flush deepened, then he laughed. "I'm being punished," he said. "Terry told me that if he caught me carrying a gun he'd run me out of western Utah."* His mouth twisted in wry self-appraisal. "I'm always getting in trouble. I can't keep my big mouth shut."

English returned the grin, but his lacked humor. He was thinking that Youngman's description might well fit himself. His fight would certainly attract the attention he had not wanted. The fewer people who were interested in his movements, the more chance he'd have of carrying out Seward's orders.

But it was too late for regrets.

"You're a marked man," Youngman said. "You're the Chief of the Washoe. Every bad man in the territory will be itching to meet the man who whipped Sam Brown. And Sam won't leave you alone. As soon as he's up he'll gather his crew and hunt you out. You've either got to leave the mountain or have friends."

English offered no comment. The boy's sensitive face frowned thoughtfully. "If you weren't a Yankee . . ." Something in the way he said it annoyed English.

"I was born in Virginia." He did not add that his family had moved to New York when he was less than a year old.

Vance Youngman's face cleared. "Then it's

*Nevada was part of Brigham Young's Utah Territory Until 1861.

easy. We'll talk to Terry; once you're with the judge, Sam Brown won't dare lay a dirty finger on you."

English temporized. He had had no thought of following Burke's careless suggestion that he join the Southern forces and learn their plans for himself. He found the very thought of acting as a spy highly distasteful. "I didn't notice that Sam Brown was impressed by your talk of Terry."

The boy's wry grin returned. "That's because Brown knows I'm in bad with the judge. He knows that Terry has ordered me not to carry a gun, and Brown was drunk tonight. But make no mistake, he takes his orders from Terry, and if Terry tells him to leave you alone he will."

English shrugged. "If Sam Brown is a fair sample of Terry's crowd, I'd feel safer without their protection."

The boy stared at him, then he laughed. "Don't judge Terry by Sam Brown. Terry's a gentleman, a general. Wait until you meet him and you'll change your mind. He's born to lead, born to command."

"And why should he interest himself in me?"

"Why not?" Vance Youngman fairly bubbled with enthusiasm. "You're southern born, and you can fight. We need fighters. Come with us and your fortune is made. We're going to seize the mines at the first sign of war. We'll work them for the South, and after the South wins we're to be the owners. We have Terry's word for that. Which mine do you want, the Ophir, the Gould and Curry, the Mexican . . . ? Take your choice. Serve Terry and you'll be rich past all your dreams."

English stared at the boy. Either Vance Youngman was mad, or Terry was mad, or both; to plan to seize the greatest mining camp in the world, to run off its lawful owners and allot the riches with the free hand of a grateful emperor. What kind of man was this Terry?

"Perhaps I should meet him," English said, slowly.

"Of course." The boy came from his place on the bed.

"I'm riding to Carson to meet him now. I should have been gone an hour ago. Come with me. Let me tell Terry what you did to Brown. I won't leave you here alone and unprotected."

Chapter Five

The city which had been named for Frémont's frontier guide was not yet a city. Laid out originally as Eagle Hot Springs, it had been renamed two years before and was fast supplanting Genoa as the unofficial capital of western Utah.

Their rented horses carried them along the crowded road at a good clip. It was after midnight, but still the wagons moved, ferrying their never ending cargos of supplies.

It was startling to cross the high desert valley through the barren empty land on a road where you were never out of sight of other travelers.

Carson's main street was the busy trail, but the side thoroughfares were dark and deserted at this hour. Youngman turned his horse into the second of these and led the way to its further end, where a figure came silently out of the gloom and after a muttered word took their mounts away.

The unpaved path was thick with dust and it was so dark here that English could barely see his companion as the boy moved toward a door at the rear of the frame house.

Before the door Youngman halted on a slab-like stone and knocked, his knuckles making a hollow sound on the wide panel as he gave three long raps, then two short ones. They waited. The stillness was broken only by the distant whining grind of the ungreased freight wagons.

The door opened suddenly, no light beyond it. English sensed rather than saw that a man stood in the dark rectangle. He did not speak.

Then Youngman's voice, clear, yet low-pitched, broke the tension of waiting. "The Circle is complete. It embraces everything."

A deep, rumbling tone answered him. "And of what is this Circle made?"

"Of gold, what else?"

"Enter, Sir Knight," The unseen man's voice eased as if he had recognized a friend, and an inner door swung open bathing the hall with yellow lamplight.

In its glow Ken had his first look at the door guard, a big man in the rough dress of a miner, and in that same instant the man saw him.

His voice tightened and the gun he was lowering lifted again. "Who's with you, Vance?"

"A friend," said Youngman eagerly. "A Virginian. He licked Sam Brown. You should have seen the fight, Crowford."

The guard did not share Youngman's excitement. "You know the rule." His tone was a warning. "No strangers." His dark accusing eyes probed at English. Ken's quick ear caught the rustle of sound on the path behind him, and he guessed that the man who had stabled their horses was at his back.

When Youngman had suggested that he ride to Carson to meet Judge Terry it had not occurred to him that the boy was coming down to attend a meeting of the mysterious Knights of the Golden Circle. Had he guessed, he would not have made the ride.

Youngman might be fool enough to introduce a chance stranger at a secret meeting, but certainly not all of Terry's followers would be so easy to deceive, and unconsciously Ken's hand strayed to the butt of his revolver. The cylinder was loaded and primed with six charges and there was a spare loaded cylinder in his pocket.

But even as his questing fingers touched the stock he let his hand fall away. He was in an unknown town, and he had convincing evidence that there was no law in western Utah save what men made for themselves.

He waited, apparently untroubled and relaxed, as the man behind him moved up so close he could feel the hot breath on the back of his neck.

The door guard held his pistol ready. "See how he's armed, Joe."

English said easily, "There's a gun in my belt, a knife in my boot."

His ready words disconcerted the guard. Vance Youngman spoke with heat. "Max Crowford, I told you he's a friend of mine. Would I bring a spy into a council?"

The man in the hall wavered. "We'll let the judge decide. Walk past me, and no tricks."

English would much rather have turned the other way. He knew that he stood in far greater danger at the moment than he had when Sam Brown's dirty fingers had been locked about his throat.

But there was no turning back now. An effort to avoid facing Terry would be a sure confession of guilt, and he read in the face of the door guard a cold, clear purpose. This man, at the first hint of suspicion, would shoot him down as coolly as if he were a dog.

The room into which he came, with Youngman at his back and Crowford bringing up the rear, was big, surprisingly large when judged from the outward appearance of the house.

There were eight men standing in a tight group. They turned at the sound of his entrance, spreading a little so that no one stood between him and Terry.

There was no mistaking the ex-justice of the California supreme court. He stood a quarter of a head taller than the men around him, and there was a good two hundred and fifty pounds on his big frame, but he was not fat.

The jaw was firm, well set, the hair light brown, a little long. His eyes were imperious, open either to quick, violent rage, or ready heartfelt laughter.

Seeing him, you could not doubt his honesty, but you might well doubt his quick snap judgements.

A leader, he dominated the room and the men in it with a self-sureness which had known little denial, and after the first quick surprise at English's presence he listened to Crowford's words with unchanging expression.

Youngman broke in angrily. "I tell you," the boy said, "that this man is my friend. His name's English. He's Virginia born, and he saved my life when Sam Brown jumped me at the Silver Lode."

Terry ignored Youngman. He walked forward until he stood directly in front of English, studying every detail of the newcomer's dress, his arms, his carriage. "Who are you? Why do you come here?"

English matched his look, then let his eyes

travel around the room. The other men watched him with open hostility, but English managed just the note of surprised uncertainty.

"I seem to have stumbled into some kind of meeting. I'm sorry if my presence is unwanted. My," he hesitated for the barest instant, then added, "friend," and nodded toward the fuming Youngman, "insisted that I come here with him. He wanted me to meet Judge Terry."

"And why did you want to meet me?" Terry's questioning stare had not relaxed.

"Dammit," said Youngman. "He didn't. It was my idea. I tell you he saved my life."

Cold humor glinted in Terry's eyes. "In some quarters that might be considered an act of unimportance."

The boy's face was a dull red, but before Terry he kept his quick anger in hand. "You should thank English," he said levelly. "Brown was drunk, bragging in the saloon how we mean to take over the lode. I didn't have a gun; your orders," he added the last as if in afterthought, "but I told him to shut up, and he jumped me. I'd have a slit windpipe except for English."

"That doesn't explain bringing a stranger here." Terry's voice was coolly neutral as if he were again on the bench, judging testimony.

"What would you have done?" Vance Youngman demanded. "He just arrived this morning. He has no friends. As soon as Sam Brown recovers his wits he'll get his boys and go gunning for English."

His voice rose with passion. "You made me promise to go unarmed, to keep out of fights. I couldn't stay and help the man who saved my life protect his own, so I brought him here. If you don't want him to stay, we'll leave, but I'm warning you, if I leave, I leave the Circle. I'll strap on a gun and be my own man again."

Terry was unmoved by Youngman's outburst. He said in his full, rich voice, "You'll leave when I tell you. You took an oath, and you'll keep it." His considering eyes turned to English. "As for you," he hesitated. "I'm not ungrateful for what you did to that animal Brown. He needs a whipping now and then. I'm interested in your motives, if you weren't perhaps using Brown as a means of gaining this boy's confidence in the hope that he would do exactly what he's done."

English started to say that he had had no idea who Youngman was, or who Brown was for that matter. But he stopped. Although it was true, he had no way of proving the words, and these men were too deeply engaged to take chances.

"Well?" Terry sounded impatient.

English shrugged, "Why bother. You wouldn't believe what I said."

There was a hint of admiration in Terry's eyes. "You're a cool one," he conceded, "or perhaps you don't quite realize what you've come up against."

"I'd be entirely stupid not to guess that," English said and again glanced around the ring of watchful faces. "I heard the password given at the door. I've been hearing about the Golden Circle for months, about Lopez, waiting in Havana to organize the new Empire of the Caribbean, about the Councils which have been set up all over the country."

Someone drew a sharp breath, and glancing sidewise English found that Vance Youngman was staring at him.

Terry said, curiously, "You are remarkably well informed." There was a finality in the tone which told English that he had already been judged in the man's mind, that the verdict had gone against him.

Yet he said, easily, "No better informed than thousands of people in the East. You out here may not realize how open the filibusterers have been with their plans. I only repeat what is common knowledge beyond the Mississippi."

Terry's voice softened. Had English known the man better he would have recognized the unexpected mildness as a sign of danger.

"We aren't so ill informed as you think, Mr. English. We had word, only yesterday, a letter from Vallandingham, warning us that Senator

Seward had dispatched an agent to Washoe. We must be careful."

English was startled. He knew the Ohio congressman by sight, knew that Vallandingham was reputed to be an active leader of the Knights of the Golden Circle. But how could the fiery politician have learned of English's mission? There was only one possible source, and Seward had been careless before. Honest himself, the Senator was inclined to be too trustful of those around him.

Ken felt the muscles of his stomach contract into a tight ball. These men were gathered, plotting treason, planning rebellion. They might shrug off the suspicion of their fellow miners, but their treatment of an agent would be far different. And if Vallandingham had mentioned him by name . . .

He studied Terry's face, trying to read behind the impassive mask with which the man screened his thoughts. "So you see," the ex-judge was still speaking softly. "We can take no chance. The next few weeks are crucial to our plans. We may be doing you an injustice, Mr. English, but it is far better that we misjudge an innocent man than allow an enemy into our councils."

He waited, as if expecting a hurried protest. English kept silent.

Terry went on. "If you are what you appear to

be, a traveler, a born Southerner, come out here perhaps in search of wealth, there must be someone in Washoe who knows you, who can vouch for your being here?"

English shook his head. "As far as I know, I have no friends in the whole district."

"Isn't that a little strange?" Terry's tone now sounded musical. "Strange that a man would come clear to Sun Mountain without any friends to greet. Most of us came to Washoe because we had heard from friends or acquaintances about the mines, about the new camp. Most of us came from California, but you, by your own admission, are from the East. Would it be Washington City?"

English knew that his silence was a damning admission, but there was no defense that would convince them.

The man who had guarded the entrance sounded impatient. "Let me hang him by his thumbs. I'll bet he'll answer fast enough once his toes come clear of the floor."

"Well?" said Terry.

English shrugged, and in that moment a door opened to the right and two girls appeared. "Aren't you men ready for coffee . . . ?" The first girl stopped, staring at their intent faces, then turning her eyes toward the man on whom all attention was centered.

"Why, Mr. English." Mary Frances Everett

stepped fully into the room. "Father, why didn't you tell me that Mr. English was coming?"

Her voice broke the tension which had held the encircled men, and several of them shifted uncertainly. Terry, who seldom showed surprise, showed none now. He turned slowly, courtly as always. "Do you know Mr. English, Miss Mary?"

"Know him?" The girl looked slowly around at the silent men. "But of course I know him. Why do you ask, Judge?"

"How well do you know him? How long have you known him?"

The girl had caught the strain in the room. She looked at English, noting his still, unsmiling features. "I . . . what a question to ask a girl, Judge."

"Mary—" A short, carefully dressed man had stepped quickly forward. He was not much taller than the girl and his small body had a pudgy, well-fed look as if from careful living, but there was a resemblance to the girl and English guessed that this was her father. "Mary, this is no time for nonsense. This is highly important, very grave. We have asked Mr. English to give an account of himself, of his presence, which he has refused to do."

"Sir," English said, quietly, "I have not refused. I merely said . . ."

Terry cut him short, brusque again. "This is

serious, Miss Mary. Please be careful how you answer. You know this man, how well?"

She looked directly at English and he thought he caught a glint of mockery in her dark eyes, but when she answered her words were solemn. "Well enough so that I made the trip to Washoe with him last night on the stage."

The second girl caught her breath audibly. Mr. Everett looked as if he might have a stroke. Terry started, surprised out of his usual poise. Vance Youngman made a noise deep in his throat. The girl went on.

"I . . . I don't know what this is all about"—she made a pretty picture of confusion now—"but I can appreciate Mr. English's reticence. I believe he was protecting me."

Suddenly embarrassment replaced the hostility which had charged the room. Terry knew that he could not regain control of the situation as long as the girls were present.

Everett was gasping. Vance Youngman was staring at the floor. Terry cleared his throat. "Mr. English," he said, slowly, "I can't understand your actions here tonight, nor am I entirely satisfied, but, well, if you and the young ladies will withdraw to the next room for a few minutes."

Everett gave a convulsive gesture as if in protest, but Terry ignored him. Mary Frances seemed again to recover her composure. English checked the laughter that unaccountably rose in him, gave Terry the slightest nod, and followed the girls through the door.

Not until it had closed behind him did he draw a full breath, then he moved across the room to where Mary Frances had seated herself in a wing chair. "Why did you . . . ?"

She looked up at him. "I was listening at the door, Mr. English. I heard what was said. I didn't believe you would enjoy hanging by the thumbs."

"You're so right." He let the laughter come into his eyes. "Yet you've ruined yourself . . . I mean they'll talk and, I . . ."

"You'll make an honest woman of me?" Her lips quirked and the other girl spoke in a horrified voice. "Mary Frances!"

"Hush, Ruthie. This is business" She grinned up at him. "Don't worry about it, Mr. English. You see, I'm engaged. I'm supposed to marry Vance Youngman."

English was wholly shocked, and then he remembered her tactics on the stage. "My reprieve," he said dryly, "is going to make Mr. Youngman most uncomfortable."

"Don't be too confident of your reprieve," she said, and came to her feet, easily, like an active boy. "There's just one thing I want to know. Are you a spy, Mr. English, and if so, what are you doing in my father's house?"

Chapter Six

Ken English stared at Mary Frances, and found her mockery gone, her eyes dark and disturbed.

He said, slowly, "Please believe me, I did not come here as a spy. Had I known where Youngman was headed, I wouldn't have ridden along."

The second girl watched him uncertainly. Her resemblance to Mary Frances was marked, but she lacked the younger girl's spark of humor, and she said in a disaproving voice, "I've never in my life seen anything more disgraceful." she was speaking to her sister, ignoring English. "It's very obvious that you don't know this man nearly as well as you pretended, that you lied to Father and the judge."

"Pooh!" Mary Frances's tone was bantering again. "They're men, and men were born to be lied to. Besides, I most certainly did not lie. I told the exact, actual truth. If they chose to put a wrong interpretation on my words it's because their minds aren't as gentlemanly as their manners."

Ruth Everett looked at her sister helplessly. Six years older, she had supervised the upbringing of the younger girl. But she had never understood her sister and she did not understand her now.

"You mean that you did accompany Mr. English on the stage?"

"She means," said English. "that we rode on the same stage, not that we were together."

"We most certainly were," Mary Frances insisted, "and he saved my life. I was starving when we got to Strawberry, and he brought me food. I don't know how he got it. I suspect he must have stolen it; we were the only passengers who managed to get something to eat. Also he saved me from a whiskey drummer. If I'd had to ride one mile farther beside that alcoholic gentleman, I'd have been quite drunk from his fumes."

"Mary Frances, will you stop joking." Ruth sounded as if she had reached the end of her endurance. "Believe me, girl, this is very serious, to introduce a casual acquaintance into a Golden Circle meeting."

"I didn't introduce him," Mary Frances said,

logically. "Vance introduced him. Vance seems to think that Mr. English saved his life." She glanced sidewise at Ken. "Rather a speciality of yours, helping people in trouble."

"Now listen to me." English felt that had Ruth been wearing a thimble she would have tapped the younger girl's wrist sharply. "It's high time you began to realize that life isn't a game. Father is deeply involved with Terry and the Golden Circle. If this man," she looked at English, and suddenly her cheeks were stained with color, "if Mr. English should be a Northern spy, then Father and Judge Terry, and Doctor McMeans, yes, and Vance Youngman are likely to be hanged."

"Of course they may be hanged, but that's not Mr. English's fault." The girl sounded impatient. "If they insist on acting like a bunch of half-grown children, plotting, playing with secret societies, with handshakes and mumbled passwords, what do they expect?"

"Mary Frances! Your father's daughter, a Southern girl!"

"I'm not a Southern girl," Mary Frances told her deliberately, "and I'm not interested in a lot of stupid politics. If you and Father want to continue pretending that you still live in Georgia, that's your affair. But I was only eight years old when we came to California, and San Francisco is the only home that I really remember.

"And if you ask me," she went on, "Terry and

those men care nothing about Father. They're using him for their own purposes, but he's too flattered by Terry's patronage to realize it, and you are as flattered as he is."

"Mary . . ."

"And it's a lucky thing I decided to come to Carson. It's about time someone in this family showed a grain of intelligence."

Her sister was almost in tears. "I'll not stay here and be insulted." She turned half blindly to a door on the left and disappeared into the kitchen.

Mary Frances watched the door for an instant, then faced English, her eyes darker than he had ever seen them. "And now," she told him "it's your turn. If you are not playing in this exciting little game I suggest that you leave here quietly, forget that you were in this house or that you saw anyone at that meeting."

He started to answer, but his words were cut short by a scream. English moved faster than thought. In one jump he reached the door through which Ruth Everett had disappeared and threw it open.

Across the wide room the older sister was struggling in the grasp of a masked man. A second intruder stood in the outer doorway, holding a revolver. As English appeared the man in the doorway raised his gun and fired, the bullet striking the wall close to English's head.

English fired in return and saw the man spin away into the outer darkness.

The one who struggled with Ruth flung the girl against the stove and ripping a revolver from his belt swung to face English.

Ken was afraid to shoot because of the girl. He jumped to meet the man, knocking the heavy weapon aside as it exploded in the air, the slug tearing into the ceiling.

The man ducked, dropping to his knee as he lost his gun, and drew a knife in its place, then came up with the agility of a cat. He struck, but Ken's thick coat caught the thrust, turning the knife partly so that the sharp point only plowed a channel between his ribs, stinging, hard and burning.

Ken dropped his own gun, seized the man's wrist, brought up his knee and smashing down the forearm across the bone of his thigh, broke it.

The man's high cry was shrill with fear and pain. The knife slid from his nerveless fingers and clattered to the floor. He twisted, ducking backward as the outer door was again filled by an armed man.

Mary Frances' warning cry dropped English to his knees, and the following shot went over his head. He clawed for his own gun as the knife wielder scuttled for safety, disappearing into the darkness, covered by the armed man who held the door.

Ken had his gun now and managed a shot and saw that the door was suddenly empty, and heard the beat of savage shouts from outside, telling that Terry's followers had scrambled through the other exit to join the fight.

He put his hand to the floor to boost himself, and felt the boards wet and sticky under his fingers. He looked down dazedly and saw the blood, and slowly realized that it came from the knife hole in his side.

He tried to rise and was surprised that his legs refused to lift him, and then the room filled up with clamoring men and he heard Terry saying angrily above the confusion, "Where's English? The damn spy led his friends directly to this meeting. I hope he didn't get away."

Mary Frances had been bending over English in an effort to help him rise. Her back was to Terry, and her body blocked his view of the fallen man.

She straightened stiffly, tense with gathering anger. "You belabor the wrong man, Judge Terry. It was you who led this fight here, who endangered all our lives by bringing your theatric intrigues to this house. You should be thankful to Mr. English. But for him, you'd all be prisoners. He's the one who got hurt. Doctor McMeans, he needs your help." She stepped aside so that Terry could see English on the floor.

Terry stared downward, his face reddening slowly, then he motioned the doctor forward and turning, left the house without a word.

Chapter Seven

English had the confused sensation of being lifted, of crying out once when a hand touched his burning side, then everything became misty and through the gathering fog he heard someone say, "He's passed out."

He wanted to tell them that he had not passed out, that never in his life had he passed out. But his lips were stiff and inflexible.

He thought, A little knife wound wouldn't do this to me. It must be the beating Sam Brown gave me earlier.

He heard the murmur of voices. They seemed to go away, and finally a shirt-sleeved man was bending over him and a strange voice said, "He's lost a lot of blood, but the knife struck no vital organ, and he seems very strong. In a week he should be on his feet. No, Miss Mary, he's not going to die of this. He'll probably live to hang yet."

English slept. When he came awake, sunlight was flooding a room fresh with chintz and lace curtains. He opened his eyes tiredly and studied his surroundings. After the spartan bareness of the hotel this room seemed warm and homelike, a woman's room, but he was washed out and had little interest.

Then he turned his head and saw her. Ruth Everett sat beside the window, an embroidery frame on her knee. But her slender hands were idle as she stared out toward the high, snow-capped mountains. Her face was in repose, smooth and pretty with a quietness which spoke of internal peace. Nothing fiery here; hers was a quiet, trustful innocence which had beauty in itself.

He had a long moment to study her before she realized that he was awake and turned, her cheeks staining slowly.

"You—you're feeling better?"

He managed to say, "Much better," which was a lie. He was terribly weak, almost helpless, and his side burned as if it were pressed by a hot coal.

She rose then and moved out of the room, returning with a bowl of soup, rich with meat broth. It tasted at the moment better than anything he had ever eaten.

She fed him, since he was not able to feed himself, and the action gave him an acute sense of embarrassment. He was not a man who had had much waiting on, and he resented the weakness which made it impossible for him to help himself. But when he tried to say this she checked him by placing her fingers against his hot forehead. They were curiously cool, wonderfully soothing, and in a few moments he was again asleep.

When he roused for the second time Mary Frances was in her sister's chair. A lamp burned on the table and she was reading from a smudged newspaper, smiling a little.

It gave him a chance to judge the difference between these girls. Even in repose Mary Frances' face had a quick animation. Her cheeks were thinner, and lacked the peach-and-cream softness of Ruth's complexion.

Mary Frances would never be entirely still, completely relaxed.

She glanced up from her reading as if drawn by the power of his questing eyes.

"Well, well, the hero is awake."

He managed a wry grin.

She said, "You aren't acting according to type. You are supposed to rise on one elbow and demand wildly, "Where am I?"

"Well," he said, weakly, "where am I?"

"That's better." Her face looked severely serious, but there was again the leavening spark in her dark eyes. "You are in my sister's room and Ruthie is horrified for fear you may catch sight of her lace underpants or something equally personal. This whole business has been a terrible shock to Ruth. She's convinced that the ruffian would have strangled her had you not dashed to the rescue. She's both delighted and upset by your presence in her bed."

His lips smiled despite his weakness. "It doesn't seem to trouble you."

"Why should it?" She tossed her head so that the dark curls at the nape of her small round neck danced. "You aren't in my bed, and you aren't my spy."

"So now I'm a spy again?"

"Aren't you? You talked last night in your delirium, about Burke, and about what a fool Seward is." She saw the quick alarm in his eyes and smiled purposefully. "I haven't told anyone yet, but it puts you in a rather uncomfortable position, doesn't it, Mr. English?"

Again he managed to smile wryly. "Almost as uncomfortable as your own, unless you've changed sides since last night."

She looked at him thoughtfully. "Make no mistake, I am not in sympathy with Judge Terry and those fools he leads, but I intend to protect my father. Can you give me a good reason why I shouldn't turn you over to them to be hanged?"

He was not perturbed. "I only wonder that you've waited this long."

She pursed her lips as if angrily. "That wouldn't have been fair, not after the way you came to Ruth's aid. Besides, you present something of a riddle. Undoubtedly you were sent here by Seward, and yet last night you fought Burke's firemen."

He managed to raise himself on his elbow.

She came out of the chair in one easy movement and was beside the bed, forcing him to lie down. "Men have no sense at all," she complained. "How do you expect to regain your strength when you keep popping up like a jumping jack?"

For some reason her action infuriated him. He was so helpless, so overwhelmingly weak. Two drops of moisture forced their way from under his eyelids. He knew he was crying and the knowledge increased his anger. It had been a long time since he had cried. It took time to control his voice, time until he could ask, "What did you say, about Burke's men I mean?"

"Didn't you realize it was Burke's firemen you fought last night?"

"How could I know?"

She studied him with a long silent stare. "No,

I guess you didn't. You wouldn't fight your own crowd that way."

He said, painfully, "I still don't believe it was Burke's men, to break into a private house like a bunch of hoodlums."

She considered him again. "Either you are a great actor, or you are a tremendous fool and I don't know which, but either way this bed makes a very passable prison and I think I will just keep you here until I decide."

She turned and went out, shutting the door, not too gently, leaving Ken English madder than he had ever been at anyone in his life.

Chapter Eight

Tom Burke, sitting in the company office behind the Hook and Ladder Fire House, stared at the dozen men grouped before him and tried to find words with which to lash them.

The office was a cluttered place, filled with uniforms, and spare leather buckets, and the set of special axes which Burke had personally freighted from San Francisco. On the wall behind the table was a full-length picture of Burke, in gala uniform, holding his trumpet in his right hand and looking down with stern unrelenting eyes.

But the eyes in the picture were no more fierce than the ones which the chief engineer turned on his cringing followers.

"Bunglers," he shouted, "idiots. How many

times have I told you not to make an open break? We aren't strong enough, and well you know it. The secesh could sweep us from the mountain if they took it into their heads. What would we use for muskets?" His eyes centered on a small man who carried his right arm in a neat sling.

"You, Cardise. It was your idea to follow Vance Youngman to Carson last night?"

Cardise stirred unhappily. "We had Terry," he muttered, "and McMeans, and the rest of their leaders. If it hadn't been for that stranger, the one who beat Sam Brown . . . I was in the kitchen. We'd have taken them by surprise, but . . ."

"But you didn't," Burke was checking his anger with obvious difficulty. "You got a broken arm instead. How many more got hurt?"

Cardise answered unwillingly, "Hammond has a ball in his shoulder, Mike Borhn got creased. Julia's taking care of them."

"And what happened to this man English?"

Cardise shook his head. "We don't know. I've had the boys watching for him at the hotel. He didn't come back there."

Burke rose. In the small room he towered above them. "And why are you watching for him?"

Cardise's mouth turned ugly. "What do you expect us to do? If we find him we'll . . ."

"You'll do nothing." Burke was savage and they knew that it was dangerous to cross him when he was in this mood. "You will let him alone until I tell you otherwise. Is that understood?"

They grumbled, shifting their feet on the rough boards.

His eyes glared at them from under the heavy brows. "I can lick any man here." It was a flat statement. "And the next one of you who doesn't follow orders will be hanging from the nearest mine headframe. Now, about this English . . ."

"Maybe he's dead." Cardise sounded hopeful. "I put a knife into his side."

"Get out," said Burke. "I should turn you loose and let the secesh finish you. It's what you deserve. Get out, and don't let me hear of any brawling until I give the word."

He watched them jam through the door, relieved to escape so lightly. No one knew exactly what Tom Burke would do. At times he had knocked a fireman insensible merely for failing to work the pump properly. An explosive man, Burke, but honest, a leader, one whom they followed, even though they feared him.

Alone in the room he paced heavily to the window and stared up the street toward the working pit of the Ophir. He saw George Hearst talking to Bill Stewart and turned away. He felt a million years old for all that he was still under thirty. His eyes searched the rough mountain and gradually his frown relaxed as he noted the beehive activity.

He owned not one share of stock in the rich mines, but in some respects he represented the camp more thoroughly than the men who were already growing rich from the dazzling storehouse.

His life was here, dedicated to the mountain, to the town, and to the state which was not yet born. He wanted nothing save the privilege of dressing in his red fireman's shirt, of leading his volunteers in their mad dash to smother any blaze which threatened the camp, for he hated blindly anything that endangered this growing city.

Tom Burke had been a soldier, a wanderer, a saloon brawler, drifting from one spot to the next, one rush to the next, always searching for something which seemed to escape him.

But here in the rugged Washoe mountains, above the hot barrenness of the desert sinks, he had come home. He loved Sun Mountain without reason, as some men give their love to gold, as others abandon all for women.

Firmly he believed that this town of shacks which struggled in uneven lines across the rocky shelfs of the forbidding canyon was destined to become one of the great cities of the world. He desired this, was willing to fight for its accomplishment with all the force of his passionate nature.

And in a lesser degree he held the same blind loyalty to the Union. He was not an educated man and he did not stop to analyze the forces which were driving the nation toward civil war. He knew only that Judge Terry and those who followed him were striving to break up the country, were threatening Sun Mountain, Virginia City, Gold Hill, and the satellite camps in the valley below.

Burke was a realist, recognizing danger, ruthless in his thinking, and had he had sufficient strength he would have seized Terry and the rest of the Southern leaders and hung them joyfully. It was not squeamishness which made him wait, nor any fear of retroactive action by the law. It was rather a canny caution which made him weigh his strength against that of the enemy, and like a clever general hold his hand to choose the time and place of battle when the odds would favor his side.

In a sense he realized that he and Terry were both in the same position, for despite the brags of the Southerners, despite their stone forts and their eighty muskets, they were as weak in their way as was Burke. And Terry, like Burke, held his hand, not from choice, but because he hesitated to risk a decisive battle, not knowing for certain his own strength, nor that of his enemy.

There were some twenty thousand men in the district, miners, ranchers, speculators, all of whom had come to the mountain in search of wealth. How would these men act when the crisis came? Would they fight for the Union, for the South, or would they stand aside and let Terry and Burke and their close followers battle out the issue uninterrupted?

That was the question which held Tom Burke silent but restless on this spring morning, while a mile away in one of his forts, Terry debated the same issue.

"It seems," he said, rubbing his bearded chin with the heel of a hand, "that Burke and his damn firemen are about ready to step into the open. If they weren't sure of their strength, they'd never have dared attack us last night."

"They failed," said Vance Youngman. "We beat them."

Terry looked at the boy without liking. Hotheaded and impetuous himself, he still had little sympathy with that failing in others.

"Did we? We were nicely surprised. They seized the horse guard and trussed him up before he ever guessed they were within miles. It was a bad break for them that Miss Ruth entered the kitchen. Had the room been empty they'd have had us before anyone could pull a gun.

That man English delayed them long enough for us to get into the yard."

"I'm still not certain about him," said McMeans.

"Nor I," Terry admitted, "but he fought Burke's men, and they knifed him which would hardly have happened if he is Seward's spy." He turned to the man who had guarded the house door. "What did you find out, Crowford?"

"Very little." The man's gravel voice was sullen. "I talked to the people at the hotel. They know nothing except that he arrived on the Placerville stage yesterday morning. I searched his duffle, nothing there, but there wouldn't be if he is an agent."

The room was filled with thoughtful silence which Vance Youngman broke by saying, "I don't think we should leave him at Everett's. I think we should move him from there."

Crowford said, heavily, "You're the man that took him to Carson in the first place."

Youngman's thin face was sullen. "I guess I made a mistake."

Doctor McMeans turned to study him. "Are you worried because you're afraid he is a spy, or because he has some acquaintance with your girl?"

"Damn you!" Youngman's face flushed hotly and he started forward.

Terry was suddenly red with anger. He thrust

out a heavy hand and catching the boy's shoulder spun him backward against the wall. "I'll have no brawling. Stop it."

Youngman was so mad that he almost sobbed. "Then make him apologize to Mary Frances."

Terry controlled his raging temper with a visible effort. "Am I to have nothing but fools around me always? He only repeated what the girl said herself. We've got more important things to worry about than your love affairs. As for moving English, I prefer to have him stay. At least we know where he is, and Everett is loyal, even if he is a pompous idiot."

Youngman's face was still red, his eyes savage. He stared at Terry for one long moment as if tempted to jump at the judge's throat, then without speaking he swung to the door and went out, slamming it behind him.

Terry gazed at the shaking panels. He sighed as if suddenly very weary and his big shoulders stooped a little. "I'm afraid we're in for trouble with that one."

"He's an ass," Crowford admitted, "but I'm not sure he isn't right. We should get that spy out of the Everett house. Everett isn't very smart, as you said a minute ago, and we need him. His stores are the perfect front to cover our shipments of powder and ball. This English is glib. No telling, he might talk Everett into changing sides."

Terry considered in silence, not rejecting the man's words, yet not ready to agree. "So what do you think should be done?"

Crowford grinned, showing irregular teeth. "If you leave it to me, I'll haul him back to the hotel and send word to Sam Brown that you don't care what happens. Brown will take care of the rest. They're laughing at him in every saloon on the lode. He's fit to be tied. He's sharpening that sixteen-inch butcher knife and panting for a chance to carve English into small pieces."

Terry shook his head. He was as ruthless as Burke, but from the first his legal mind had insisted that they back up their actions by law. To this end he had Circle members file claims to the east and west of the lode. In their name he had brought suit against the mine owners, intending to bribe the judges at the territorial court at Genoa to find in his favor.

Once these court orders were in his hands, he could have his Circle members deputized, serve the papers, and take possession of the whole lode.

He realized that although a good percentage of Sun Mountain's citizens were Southern in their politics, they were still honest men who would object to the outright theft of the mining property.

"Keep Brown out of this," he warned. "That murderer will cause us more trouble than you know. There isn't a decent man in the territory who doesn't hate him."

Crowford stared at his leader. He opened his bearded lips to argue, thought better of it, and turning, left the room.

Chapter Nine

For four days Ruth Everett mothered English in her fluffy room, but he saw nothing of the younger girl and her marked neglect filled him with concern. Had she denounced him to Terry? Were they holding him prisoner here? What had happened in the east? The inauguration day had passed.

On the fourth evening Mary Frances came into the room and he watched her keenly as she stopped beside the bed.

"You look very healthy for a dying man."

"It's the nursing and the food," he told her. "Nobody could stay sick under your sister's care. I'd have starved to death three days ago if I'd depended on you."

"I stayed away purposely," she told him, "to

give you a chance to think."

He looked at her, appreciating her shrewdness. "I've been thinking," he said. "You made it plain the other night that you do not approve of Terry's use of your father. If you could persuade him to withdraw from the Golden Circle . . ."

"Then you admit you're a spy."

"Say rather an observer for the new administration."

"Mr. Lincoln?"

"Seward sent me. He'll be Secretary of State. He believes that the North and the South can be brought together, and my job is to prevent an open break here at Sun Mountain until those adjustments can be made."

She laughed mockingly. "And leave Terry and Burke without a war? I'd like that, but I'm afraid it isn't possible."

He nodded. "I've found that out since I came here."

"So, we're back where we started. You're a spy and a danger to my father. You're also too well to hold in this room."

He said, meekly, "I am a problem, at that."

"You most certainly are. I should tie you up and send for Judge Terry."

"Maybe that's best." He was grinning at her now.

"And it positively isn't a laughing matter, Mr. English. You think because I'm a girl that I will be soft and let you go. But that is not the case. I can be hard-boiled as any man, and I intend to see that you are taken care of so that you can't cause us any more trouble."

He was still smiling.

"And I am not like Ruth, letting you turn my head with your compliments."

"Have I given you any compliments?"

"Well, no." She was not disconcerted. "But I know how men act, and you will start if you think it will do you any good."

Before he had a chance to answer, the door opened and John Everett came in. He frowned when he saw his younger daughter and paused uncertainly.

John Everett had prospered in the years since he had left the thin-soiled hill farm in central Georgia, and his position in California was that of a highly successful, respected merchant.

But he had never forgotten his low beginnings and it fed his vanity to be treated as an equal by the leaders of the Southern wing. Most of these men were members of well-known families, former plantation owners, political leaders. He counted himself fortunate to be welcomed into their council.

Toward the man on the bed, his manner was reserved. He felt that English was a guest, and that by his quick action English had saved Ruth from bodily harm. For both of these reasons

John Everett maintained an air of reserved tolerance, but beneath the surface he was tortured by his daughter's apparent interest in this stranger who might well be a spy. In a sense John Everett was afraid of Mary Frances. They had never been easy with each other and there was a constant hostile friction between them which had increased as the girl grew older.

Ruth was different. He could talk to Ruth. She was trustworthy and he knew exactly how she would react in any given situation, but with Mary Frances he never knew where he stood. One instant she was defying his authority, the next making fun of him.

Yet he knew that she loved him deeply and he held for her a fierce protective passion which he had never felt for his more placid daughter.

He bowed a little as he came into the room. He liked to practice the niceties of manner which he considered were the attributes of a gentleman, never guessing that his contrived gestures made him the butt of a hundred jokes among his associates.

"Good evening. I trust you are better?" He had a disagreeable task and he was being more than polite.

English nodded, studying the small man. It was incredible to him that this pompous little person could be Mary Frances' father. He had taken Everett's measure at their first meeting and he had seen nothing in the last four days to change his opinion.

Everett was nervous. He had come to a decision, and he meant to speak his mind, but he felt slightly guilty when he met his daughter's questioning eyes. "I'd like to speak to Mr. English alone."

Mary Frances knew that he was up to something. The signs were very plain and her father had never been successful at dissembling. She hesitated, not knowing quite what to do, then realizing that she could hardly refuse to leave, she managed to smile.

"I was just going to get his supper," she said, and left the room.

Everett waited until the door was closed, then he pulled a chair close to the bed and sat down. He hesitated for a moment, fumbling with his breast pocket, then produced two cigars, one of which he offered English.

"I don't know what the doctor will think."

"And I don't care," said English, accepting the cigar gratefully and allowing John Everett to light it for him. It was the first tobacco he had tasted since entering this house, and he drew the satisfying smoke from the rich filler deep into his lungs.

Everett was embarrassed. At heart, despite his affectations, he was a kindly man, but he steeled himself with the thought that he must protect his daughter.

"I've been talking to the doctor. He says you are much improved and that you can be moved tomorrow without danger."

English said nothing, guessing what was passing through the smaller man's mind. Comfortable as he had been, it would be a vast relief to be up and moving, and this answered one question which had filled his mind. Did Terry intend to hold him at Carson? Apparently not.

Everett went on. "I don't know exactly how to say this."

English said, "I'm in your debt so deeply that nothing can possibly offend me."

"Well," said Everett, still hesitating, "there's no use pretending that you didn't walk in on our meeting the other night, or that some of my associates were suspicious of your presence."

English nodded.

"I owe you a good deal for coming to Ruth's aid, but my other daughter, well, she's young and impressionable."

English had the impulse to laugh. He had never met anyone less impressionable than Mary Frances. She struck him as being by far the most coolheaded of the family.

"And she came to your defense," the unhappy merchant added. "I don't know where she met you, or how well you know each other and I am not questioning you."

"Our meeting was casual," said English.

Everett gave him a wintery smile and English knew that the man thought he was lying. "That wasn't exactly what she implied."

"No," English admitted.

"And she's engaged. Mr. Youngman was quite naturally upset. In fact he came here last night with the intention of challenging you. I persuaded him that such an action on his part would only have made matters worse."

English started slightly, then settled back. So Vance Youngman wanted a duel. He held his peace and Everett went on in his quick, nervous tone.

"Vance is impetuous. It is something I trust he will outgrow, but he comes from an excellent family in South Carolina and naturally he is careful of his honor."

"Naturally," said English, not troubling to hide the irony in his voice.

Everett did not notice. "I want nothing to interfere with the plans."

English was growing restless. He thought, You are very proud, little man. You've apparently made a success, and you are flattered that your daughter is to marry into the Youngman family. You are flattered although you have reservations about the man she is to marry. But to you his family is more important than his faults.

"So," said Everett, not seeing his guest's inattention, "I have to admit that I find your presence unsettling. I dislike having to say this, but I feel it much better that we understand each other."

"Much better," English muttered. "I thank you for being honest. If you will arrange for a livery stable rig to take me back to Virginia, I'll try and leave Carson tonight."

"Not enough," said Everett, "you must also leave western Utah."

English stared at him nonplussed. His first thought was that Terry had taken this method to get him out of that part of the country, but a look at Everett's face told him this was not a move of Terry's. The merchant was obviously not liking the role he played, but he was too honest to maneuver cleverly. Whatever the motives behind this it was all of John Everett's doing, and he went on hurriedly.

"I've made inquiries about you, Mr. English. The hotel people know nothing, and I've been unable to find any businessman who knows you. It may be as Terry suspects, that you are a spy, but you did fight Burke's men." He paused, as if expecting his guest to speak, but when English stayed silent he continued.

"I prefer to believe that you are merely a fortune seeker like so many others who have rushed to Sun Mountain in the last year, yet you are no miner."

"No," said English. "There are other ways to make a fortune."

"Good." It was obvious that John Everett was relieved by the words. "That being the case I'll speak to you as one businessman to another. I offer a very simple proposition. If you will take the stage, agreeing not to return, I will give you an order on the manager of my San Francisco store in the amount of five thousand dollars."

English had an uncontrollable impulse to laugh. He thought, In the course of one short week I've certainly managed to make myself very popular. Sam Brown is thirsting for my blood. Burke, if it was his firemen I fought, most likely hates me. Terry, McMeans, and the Southern leaders regard me as a dangerous spy. Mary Frances holds me prisoner in her sister's bed, Vance Youngman wants to fight a duel, and now a hardheaded merchant is willing to pay five thousand dollars because he fears I'm a blackguard with designs on his daughter.

He wished the girl could hear this. He was certain that she would find her father's offer amusing, but it was probably better that she knew nothing about it.

His one idea was to leave this house as quietly as possible. He had no desire to bring trouble to the Everetts in return for their kindness. Nor did he take too seriously Mary Frances' threat to turn him over to Terry.

But she alone knew for certain that he was Seward's representative, and if she actually believed that he was dangerous to her father, there was no telling what she might attempt.

He was suddenly conscious that Everett awaited his reply and he said, "If you can arrange a carriage for tonight, after your daughters have retired . . ."

Hope came into the merchant's dark eyes, mingled with relief, and he said eagerly, "Then you'll take my offer."

Ken English was tempted. It would be much easier to let the man believe that he was quitting western Utah, but he found it impossible to lie.

"I'm sorry," he said, "I have business of my own in Washoe which is worth far more to me, and to others, than five thousand. However, I give you my word that I will cause no trouble for your family, provided we can arrange my departure so that no one guesses save ourselves."

Everett studied him, and for a moment Ken thought the merchant was about to refuse. Then he bowed his head. "I'd feel much safer," he said frankly, "if you were out of the territory, but since I have little choice, I'll have to accept your word. I'll have the carriage at midnight. Until then." He rose and moved tiredly from the room.

Chapter Ten

Feeling that his strength had fully returned although the knife hole in his side was still bandaged, Ken English left the hotel and walked toward Hawthorne's Public Livery.

It was early, and the night shifts coming out of the pits crowded the sidewalks with dirty men as he passed. He turned into the barn office and told the stable keeper that he wanted to ride to Chinatown, perhaps beyond.

Clyde Hawthorne was so heavy that it took real effort for him to lift himself out of the creaking chair. He made no comment, being a man too lazy to waste words when gestures would serve in their place.

He followed English from the cluttered room into the main driveway of the barn and along it to a box stall in the far corner.

"Take Sampson," he said, indicating the black. "I can tell by the way you walk that you've been a horseman. It isn't everyone I'd rent him to."

Ken saddled the animal when Hawthorne made no movement to touch the gear, and all the time he was cinching the center-fire rig around the black's expanded barrel he was conscious of the fat man's studying stare.

From this stable he and Youngman had procured their mounts on the night of their ride to Carson, and since Youngman would likely do business with those who shared his political faith, it was probable that Hawthorne was Southern in his sympathies.

It might be a mistake to come to Hawthorne for a mount for this day's ride, but Ken shrugged away the thought and slipped the bridle over the black's hammer head.

For all that Virginia City held a teaming throng, the town was so compact a man could not cloak his movements. If the Southerners wanted to check on English there was little he could do to prevent them.

But during the week since he had slipped out through the silent yard to where John Everett had the carriage waiting in the back street behind the frame house, no one had showed an obvious interest in Ken's movements.

He had kept close to the hotel, nursing his returning strength, reading the dispatch which the *Enterprise* had received by pony telling of the inauguration and the threats of withdrawal by the southern states.

Time was short now and like the rest of the camp he awaited the next dispatches with mounting tension. There had been no direct word from Seward, and English wrote the new cabinet officer two pressing letters. For the rest he paced his room, or idled in the hotel bar under the curious eyes of the other customers.

His fight with Brown had marked him and he knew that there was much speculation as to his presence, but no one questioned him directly. Brown was absent, Youngman avoided the hotel, and Terry was at Genoa.

The inactivity was more wearing than it had been at the Everett house. English knew a feeling of helplessness. He had to do something. He would rather have had direct orders from Seward, but he guessed shrewdly that the new Secretary of State would continue to hesitate until some move by the south forced him into action.

But the situation on Sun Mountain would not wait on the procrastinations of the eastern politicians. There had been a dozen street fights since the inaugural. Burke's firemen moved through the streets in groups for self-protection while the Southerners watched them angrily from the shelter of Terry's stone forts.

It was those forts which worried English, but more than the forts, he fretted about the eighty army rifles with which Terry had armed his men.

In the final showdown those rifles gave Terry his advantage, since Burke's firemen had nothing but side arms with which to oppose them.

The rifles had been withdrawn from California arsenals at the time of the Pyramid Lake battle with the Utes in the preceding year, and brought over the mountain by Colonel Hungerford to arm the volunteers, but rather than transport them back to the coast he had turned them over to Terry after the Indians' surrender.

Since they were army property, and the army now had a post at the new Fort Churchill, English reasoned that the only way he could complete his mission was to persuade Fort Churchill's commanding officer to commandeer those rifles. Such action would not prevent the war, but it might effectively stalemate the factions on Sun Mountain, giving the distant federal authorities sufficient time to act.

The morning was fresh, the black horse wanted to run, and English took pleasure in fighting it all along the road which wound down through Gold Hill to the river below.

Short of the river he passed the shacks of Chinatown and came into the main trail which led northward around Tahoe.

The traffic here was not as heavy as on the southern route which used the canyon of the American River, but there were enough wagons so that he was never free of the scream of their ungreased wheels, nor the clouds of dust flung up by the mules and the slow, plodding oxen.

The horse had long since had the fight ridden out of it and settled into a steady gait which ate up the miles, but the sun was well past the zenith before the adobe buildings of Fort Churchill rose from the plain of the foothill grade.

The military reservation spread out on both sides of the river, the parade ground within easy sight of the trail. In this, its first year, the fort maintained its look of newness and some of the officers' quarters were still under construction.

English reined his horse and slumping idly in the saddle let his questing eyes sweep hungrily over the ordered activity.

Far off across the bare rectangle a swirl of dust bellied up where a company of dragoons, their officers' spiked helmets glistening in the sun, wheeled and drew into parade line.

English watched with quickening interest, his shoulders straightening, his eye critical, stirred by nostalgic pride. Once this had been his regiment and his mouth quirked in self-bitterness. A cavalry man remained a cavalry man. It was something you did not put away from you, even though you laid aside the uniform.

Everything about the post was a poignant reminder of happier days and he had the impulse to turn his horse and ride back to the mountain, but instead he forced his mount toward the guard post.

The fort was a loose rectangle, commanded by the officers' quarters which lined across the high ground of the rising slope. To the north and east were grouped the stables, arsenal, and corrals while on the south the long row of barracks flanked the parade.

It was, English thought, complete and satisfying, and self-contained, removed by tradition and discipline and purpose from the frenzied bustle of the mining camp on Sun Mountain.

He swung down and waited while the sentry summoned the corporal, gave his name, and asking for the adjutant, followed the non-com on foot across a corner of the parade.

A second troop was saddling as they came abreast of the first stables and hearing his name called, English turned to see a red-faced hulking sergeant.

"So help me, Lieutenant English. And how are you, sir?"

Mike Lynch had English's fingers between his two ham-like hands, then he stepped back, saluting smartly.

English's mouth twisted in its half-grin. "Forget it, Mike. I don't rate it."

"And a crying shame," said Lynch, suddenly angry. "The First is not the same since you left."

The corporal had been watching open-mouthed and Lynch noticed him for the first time. "Off with you, Delaney." He turned to let his anger wash over the man. "'Tis myself will be conducting the lieutenant wherever he wants to go."

Delaney muttered under his breath, turned and stalked back to the guard post. Mike Lynch spat in the dust.

"Infantry man. And isn't that like the department, sending foot soldiers to patrol a thousand miles of trail? Hell, Lieutenant. We only have two companies from the First. What this country's coming to I'll never know."

English's grin widened. Lynch had twenty years of service and would die in uniform, but Ken said, "You can buy out, Mike. Men are making quick fortunes up there on Sun Mountain."

Lynch looked startled. "And what would I be doing, burrowing in a hole like a bloody mole? They can keep their silver and may it choke their gullets for all of me." He blew out his breath loudly to emphasize his disdain. "'Tis no fit job for a man." He broke off, squinting at English, noting his clothes.

"You aren't mining, sir. Would you be coming back in by any chance?"

English's grin was lost. "Don't be foolish,

Mike. Remember the general court."

"And how could I forget it," the Irishman said, sadly. "'Tis the shame of the army."

"Officers don't fight duels." English was bitter.

"You should have let me handle the skunk." Mike grew heated. "I'd have gut-shot him from an alley, which would have been better than he deserved and none would have been the wiser."

"That's done," said English; and then in a different tone, "Who's in command?"

"Jasper Stewart," said Lynch, and again spat in disgust. "Artillery man."

"I remember him," English nodded.

Lynch indicated the encircling hills with a sweep of his big arm. "What would we be doing with big guns in this desert—shooting at cactus? They give Stewart command when we need more dragoons. How can artillery guard the trail east to Salt Lake?"

"You always were a barracks lawyer," English hid his smile, "but when I get back east I'll speak to the War Department."

"Naw!" said Mike seriously. "Talking with them civilians never helped. You can't expect them to savvy this country, or a military problem—" He broke off, looking at English with renewed attention. "Did you say you've been east? What's the talk back there? Are those Southern sourbellies going to fight?"

"It looks like it."

Lynch ran his blunt, twisted fingers through thick red hair already beginning to shade into gray. "It ain't Christian," he muttered, "brother fighting brother. I saw enough of it in the old country."

"Well," said English, "a lot of good men will go with the South."

Mike considered him. "Does that mean you?"

English was taken by surprise. "Why me?"

"You're the man, I'm thinking, who licked Sam Brown?"

"Well, yes, but . . ."

The sergeant squinted at him. "I didn't associate the name although I heard it last week in Virginia. They said you were with Terry."

"They're wrong in that," English said. "I'm on the other side."

Mike grinned his relief. "Sure, you wouldn't be lining up against the flag, even if they took your uniform. Now, you wouldn't be here because of this Terry trouble?"

English was too startled to speak, and Mike took the pause as a sign of unwillingness. "It's not for the likes of me to be asking."

English had recovered. "Don't be silly, Mike. It's only that you took me by surprise. What made you guess?"

"'Twas easy," said the Irishman. "You wouldn't be coming to this post for just a visit after what has happened, so it had to be important, and what's more important than a coming war?"

"I only hope that Jasper Stewart sees things as plainly," English told him. "I'm in a spot, Mike. I have no real authority and my orders are indefinite, but I hate to sit by and watch the rebels seize Sun Mountain. Once they get control it will take a full campaign to dislodge them, and I think the Union will need all its men for other duties."

The sergeant nodded slowly. "'Tis the devil's own country for fighting," he admitted, "but what do you hope to get here?"

"Terry's rifles," English told him promptly. "The Southerners have eighty army rifles, and with them the Golden Circle can control the whole Washoe district. Without them, Terry will be no stronger than Tom Burke and his Union firemen."

Lynch had been listening thoughtfully. "And you expect Stewart to grab those guns?"

"I hope he will. After all, they are army property."

The Irishman spat. "I'm not the one to advise you, you were in the service long enough to know yourself. If you were in Stewart's shoes, would you do it without orders?"

English started to answer, then hesitated. "Well," he said, honestly, "it would depend on circumstances."

"It won't with Stewart." The old sergeant spoke with deep knowledge of the man. "He's a great one for regulations, Stewart, and rules. He was sent here to guard the trail against the Utes. He's going to tell you that, and he's going to tell you that the army ain't a police force."

English nodded slowly. "I'm afraid you may be right, Mike."

"You know I'm right," said Mike. "You knew it before you came."

"But I had to come," English said, soberly. "There are times when a man hasn't much choice. He has to try, even when he's sure there's not much chance." He was silent for a moment, then his face brightened a little. "Who's the adjutant? Maybe I can get him to see how important it is to get those guns out of Terry's hands. If I can convince him, he might help me with Stewart."

Mike Lynch's weathered face turned blank, unreadable. His voice was toneless as he said, "You'll get no help there either. The adjutant is Fred Crouse."

For a full minute English was entirely still. These three years he had known that somewhere, somehow, he and Crouse must meet, but he had not expected that meeting to take place at this newest outpost on the nation's far-flung frontier.

"So be it." His words were soft, directed more

to himself than to the man at his side.

Lynch's voice turned urgent. "You'll get no help from Crouse. He hates you. He's lived with that hate three years. You can read it in his eyes."

English looked at his former sergeant. "How long has he been with the First?"

"He joined us at Benicia Barracks, before we came over the mountains. Stay away from him, sir. It will do no good. Ride out. Forget you ever came here."

English looked at him sharply. "Has Fred been giving you a rough time, Mike?"

"He knows I'm your friend," the Irishman said, proudly. "But there never was a lieutenant I couldn't handle."

"I've got to see him."

Mike Lynch shrugged. Without further word he led the way across the parade and into a narrow-windowed room which was cool and semi-dark, the thick adobe walls cutting out the heat of the late afternoon.

The officer bending over the far desk had his blouse buttoned to its high collar. He did not look up as they entered and Lynch, after a glance in his direction, turned to the enlisted clerk.

"A civilian to see the adjutant." He did not mention English's name, as if unwilling to utter it within this room. Then he executed a smart about-face and left without a word to Ken.

English started toward the clerk, then stopped as Fred Crouse looked up, and Ken stopped, staring directly into the dark eyes of the man who had promised to kill him on sight.

Chapter Eleven

Fred Crouse was nearly as tall as English, but his body still held an adolescent thinness. His hair was dark and soft, and waved back from the high forehead. His features were small, all except the nose which jutted out from between his dark eyes as if it had been an afterthought.

The mouth was softly molded and would have given the whole face a womanish cast without the counter-balance of the nose.

The shock of seeing English tightened his lips and crystallized his eyes until they looked like dark glass. He sat for an instant, too stunned to move, his big, knob-knuckled hands balling on the pile of orders he had been signing, tightening on the pen until it snapped.

The snap of the breaking pen shattered the paralysis which gripped him.

"English!"

Ken did not speak. Although forewarned by Lynch, he too was held by shock. The boy behind the desk had changed in three years, aged until he was a mirror of his dead brother. To English it was like peering into the past and finding himself face to face with a scene from his own youth.

Even in the motion of rising Crouse used the flat of his hands to push against the desk top. It had been an old habit of Paul's to thus raise himself, and English almost cried out in involuntary protest.

"Damn you," said the boy, and came around the desk. He was not wearing side arms. Had he been, he would have shot English without hesitation. For three years English had considered the possibility of such a meeting, yet he was still unprepared for the surge of emotion which rose through him at sight of the boy.

"I'm sorry, Fred," in spite of his resolve, his voice shook a little, "I didn't come here from choice."

"Then why?" The boy was steadying himself, one hand on the corner of the desk.

"I have to see Jasper Stewart."

"It must be damned important to make you step foot on an army post." He said this grudgingly.

"It is," said English, and watched the indecision on Fred Crouse's face. The boy, he thought, is so very like Paul, the same eyes and mouth. It's the mouth that shows their weakness. Why didn't I realize that long ago? Paul Crouse was not meant to command. He cracked under his first real decision. This boy is the same. It shows in the way he hesitates, in the way he glances for help to the enlisted clerk.

Crouse's tone was uneven as he spoke to the corporal. "Will you ask Captain Stewart to step this way. He should still be in his quarters. It lacks a good twenty minutes until retreat."

The clerk who had been watching them rose and disappeared without a word, leaving them alone in the narrow room, pressed in by tragedy.

The silence between them rode up and became screamingly oppressive. Once they had been more than friends, for it was in the Crouse home that English had found a welcome he had never otherwise known. But that was gone, wiped out by violence and death, and in the younger man hero worship had turned into a fiery hate so strong that only his rigid training kept his fingers from English's throat.

Jasper Stewart came hurriedly, and was still fastening his belt as he crossed the threshold. Not a young man, Stewart. His sideburns held their touch of gray; a precise man, observing the letter of the rule, the niceties of military conduct, even on the frontier.

He bowed a little as he came in, half blinded from the glare of the western sun, and Ken knew that for the moment Stewart did not recognize him.

He had that moment then to study the older man's face, to try and formulate his appeal. Habit was very strong and this man, for all his faults, was the commanding officer. The respect in English's manner was not for Stewart but for the office which he held.

He steeled himself against the contempt in Stewart's eyes as the delayed recognition came. "Mr. English. This is a surprise." All the weight and judgment of the army condemnation was in the tone, and English felt his own anger rise as he added stiffly, "And not a pleasant one for you."

"No," said Stewart, "not a pleasant one." He glanced at Crouse, noting the boy's white, strained face, the stiffness with which he held himself, and for an instant Stewart's gray eyes were softened by compassion. Then they hardened as he looked back at English.

"I assume this visit is not a social one?"

Ken English was trying desperately to think. He knew army procedure so thoroughly. He understood the small jealousies, the petty touchiness with which service protocol is built.

He had no desire to offend Stewart, but it was

of the utmost importance that Terry's power be nullified. He spoke then with a formality which was not natural, trying to clarify each point as if writing it into a report.

By effort he held his tone level, devoid of personal feeling. "I came here," he said, "at the behest of members of the new administration to check the rumors of unrest on Sun Mountain.

"What I found both surprised and frightened me. Before I had been in the territory twenty-four hours I learned that the Southern sympathizers are near open rebellion. I learned that they have an active chapter of the Knights of the Golden Circle, that they have built forts on the lode itself, and that they are in possession of eighty government rifles."

Stewart showed his impatience. "We are aware of all that, Mr. English . . ."

"Are you aware that Judge Terry holds a commission signed by Jeff Davis, that as soon as war comes he means to take the territory, throw out the legal owners of the mines, and use Sun Mountain silver to finance the coming rebellion?"

"I am not," said Stewart icily. "You are not the first person to come here complaining of Terry and his activities. My answer to you must be the same as it was to Mr. Burke and his friends. If what you say is true, it should be the concern of the territorial authorities in Salt Lake. This fort was placed here to guard the trail against the Indians, not to police the squabbles of a mining camp."

"At least those rifles are government property. You would be perfectly within your rights in asking for their return."

"Are you instructing me in my duty, Mr. English?"

Ken flushed. "No, sir, but . . ."

"Then, since you have intimated that you have connections in Washington, may I suggest that you take up the matter there, or failing that, approach General Johnston in San Francisco. Good day." He turned abruptly on his heel and left the building before English could answer.

For an instant Ken stared at the empty door, then glanced at Fred Crouse, and was surprised to find the boy's eyes not as hard as they had been, surprised when Crouse said, evenly, "I still hate you, but I realize now that you are being punished much more effectively than you would be by dying. I watched you writhe under Stewart's contempt. I know that you will be accorded the same welcome at any army post in the land. I shall make it my business to see that everyone in the territory is familiar with your crime." He turned and picking up his helmet from the desk, fitted the strap in place and moved past English to the parade beyond the door.

For minutes English stood motionless in the narrow confines of the room, tasting the searing bitterness of the boy's words, then he turned and stepped into the open.

The sun had dropped until the western peaks threw their long shadows completely across the parade. He paused, watching the companies from their ranks, and then the haunting strains of retreat beat across the hot, windless air.

Unconsciously English removed his hat and stood stockstill, watching the colors come slowly down the staff. A lump rose in his throat, for he had the sudden instinct that this scene was symbolic and he wondered, as he saw the ranks wheel and break toward the stables, how long it would be before the flag came down over this desert land for the last time. The troop streamed past him by two's. The creak of leather, the hoarse calls of the sergeants, the smell of dust and sweat in the air all brought their memories. This was a portion of his life not likely to return. He was set aside from what he had been trained for, cut off, discarded, unwanted.

He plodded toward the gate where Mike Lynch held his horse. The sergeant's shrewd eyes read the story from English's face.

"Rough?"

"Very rough," said Ken bitterly. "You told me, but I had to try."

"Yes," said Mike. "I knew that when you came in. That's your trouble, Lieutenant. You aren't content to let things work their way through channels. You thought you could help Paul Crouse. 'Twas how you managed your own ruin."

English steadied his voice. "Forget it, Mike. That's past and done, and beyond help."

"No," said Mike. "Nothing's ever completely done."

"I said forget it. I've got other things to think about. Time's pressing me. There's no chance to appeal to Washington. And as for General Johnston . . ." He was thinking aloud. "At best he's in sympathy with Terry, at worst he could be a member of the Golden Circle."

Mike Lynch studied his face, not liking what he saw there. "Careful, Lieutenant, you're only one man."

"Sometimes," said English, still thinking aloud, "one man can be more effective than a company."

Chapter Twelve

Sandy Bowers was giving a party. In all the world a more hospitable man than Sandy Bowers would have been hard to find.

Vance Youngman had rented a carriage for the occasion to squire both Everett sisters.

For a week Youngman and Mary Frances had barely spoken to each other, and Vance was still nursing his jealousy as he drove the matched team down the side street and turned up the main trail toward the hotel at Hot Springs.

He still resented bitterly English's stay at the Everett house.

Mary Frances, with a wisdom beyond her years, was content to let him alone in his silence, but Ruth's perceptions were not as sharp, and she was unconscious of Youngman's continued ill-humor.

She chatted lightly as the team picked its way briskly around the slower freight wagons. It was the first really warm evening of the season and Ruth was in good spirits. Finally her talk turned to English and she said, "Have you seen him since he returned to Virginia?"

Youngman shook his head.

Ruth's voice was puzzled. "There was something very strange about his leaving, to slip out without a word, and he seemed so courteous and gentlemanly. I simply can't understand his being rude."

Mary Frances thought that she could. "Perhaps he was afraid. Maybe he thought we were holding him prisoner."

The older girl turned to look at her. "How absurd. Why should he think a thing like that?"

"Well," said Mary Frances. "He certainly sneaked away like an escaping highwayman."

"I don't care," Ruth told them. "I'm certain that he wasn't purposely rude. Something we don't know about must have happened."

Youngman could stay silent no longer. "Why don't you ask Mary Frances?" His tone was nasty. "She's such a dear friend of his. She must know why he ran away."

"Vance!"

He took no warning from her tone. He wanted to hurt her as he had been hurt. "Well, you boasted before those men about coming here with English on the stage."

"And you ought to thank me." Her voice was cutting. "You most certainly ought to thank me. You brought him to the house and your crowd was going to hang him by his thumbs. If I hadn't spoken they would have."

His anger turned uncertain in the gust of her rising temper. He was never a match for her, and he knew it, and he resented her ability to always put him in the wrong.

"Well," he said, sullenly, "how did you expect me to guess that you were lying? I thought you actually knew him and . . ."

"And I most certainly did." Her brown eyes sparkled in the moonlight. "You ask Ruth. Hadn't I met him, Ruthie?"

The older sister looked from one to the other. "What are you two quarreling about?" she asked bewilderedly. "I just never know what you are trying to prove."

Mary Frances wasn't quite certain herself. She was angry with Vance, and it seemed to her that the time had come to punish him. He had been acting like a small boy quite long enough.

"You know very well," she told her sister, "that Mr. English bought me supper at Strawberry, and that he rode beside me in the coach from the crest to Carson City. I guess that makes him a friend."

"Maybe you don't know him as well as you think," Vance grumbled. "We're sure he's the spy Seward sent here. I'm convinced that he fought Sam Brown purposely to make my acquaintance, hoping to get into a Golden Circle meeting."

"Vance!"

"You listen to me." His voice turned shrill. "I'm not the only one who thinks so. Max Crowford is certain, and so is Terry, and Doctor McMeans. . . ."

"And I suppose you're proud that you could be so easily used?"

"But he . . ."

"And it's not the thing for you to say about a man who took your beating."

"Listen to me . . ."

"And you'd have been in a positively bad pickle if he hadn't come to your aid."

The boy squirmed. He could not strike the girl, so he raised his whip and lashed the horses into a trot. "I wouldn't have needed his help," he muttered between his teeth, "if I'd had a gun."

"And that's another thing," she badgered him. "Do you have to let Judge Terry run your entire life?"

"He's the leader. . . ."

"And I'm not at all certain I want to marry a

man who is willing to follow blind orders. . . ."

"Even your father takes Terry's orders."

The truth of the last statement struck Mary Frances dumb, and Vance seized the opportunity to change the subject.

"I hope Sandy Bowers hasn't invited every miner and mucker on the lode here tonight."

"And who is this Sandy Bowers?"

He looked at her and shrugged. "Just a mine owner, but he's quite a character at that. He and his wife are about the only early settlers left here. Their mine is at Gold Hill, and I've heard he's already taken out a million dollars. He doesn't mind spending the money either, but they're still very common."

Ruth interrupted. "I like Mrs. Bowers. I've met her a number of times."

"Oh, Eilley's all right." Vance was being offhand. "She used to run a boardinghouse and they say she was married to a couple of Mormons before she took up with Sandy."

"It's a wonder," Mary Frances said icily, "that feeling the way you do, you'd deign to accept their invitation."

Vance turned to her in harried exasperation. "Can't I do anything to please you tonight?"

"Not when you act like a spoiled brat," she said candidly. "I don't know much about fine manners, but I've always heard that it wasn't polite to criticize your hosts when you're going to enjoy their hospitality and eat their food."

Youngman stared at her darkly for a moment, then wrapped himself in offended silence which was not broken until he turned the team into the hotel driveway.

The yard was filled with arriving guests. Carson City, despite the rawness of its many buildings, was already making pretences to culture. While the court was still held at Genoa, and the main business of the district was on Sun Mountain, the attorneys and mining men preferred to house their families in Eagle Valley where the water was sweeter and the living quieter.

Still holding his silence, Vance Youngman helped the girls from the carriage and they stood waiting beside the entrance while he drove the team back to the barn and unhitched.

The ground was hard-packed and there was little grass, but the rough hills rising behind the hotel lent a majestic dignity to the scene as the moon threw the wind-twisted trees into sharp relief.

The moon was assisted in lighting the yard by a string of gay paper lanterns which swung from a guy wire stretched between the main building and a small arbor at the far corner of the property.

To Mary Frances, fresh from San Francisco, the gathering was amazing. There were literally hundreds of people present, crowding the main public room, around the bar and the loaded tables in the dining alcove.

Sandy Bowers had starved under the desert sun, frozen in the bitter blasts which swept Sun Mountain and bore down on the huddle of wretched shacks which had then been called Mormon station.

Now that Lady Luck had embraced him he saw no reason for not sharing his good fortune with all who chose to come his way.

He bustled among his guests, clutching a champagne glass in one hand as if it were a mace of office. Pleased as a child, he greeted the sisters at the door and refusing to let them wait for Youngman, swept them toward the huge fireplace at the far end, before which Eilley Bowers was holding court.

The room was roughly barren, but the walls had been partly covered by rugs and blankets of gay design, giving the whole place a warm, homy feel.

Sandy was bubbling when he reached his wife's side. "Here's a couple of lookers. I found them out beside the door, John Everett's girls. Get them some partners, huh?"

He went happily on his way, and Eilley Bowers took over with competence. "I've got just the tickets, dearies," she winked. "Army officers, and handsome. Oh, Lieutenant Baker, Lieutenant

Crouse, looke what I've saved for you."

The officers crowded forward to be introduced and carried them off to the dance where a cadaverous man who Mary Frances thought must be at least seven feet tall was calling the squares.

Chapter Thirteen

Coming back from the barns Vance Youngman found Max Crowford leaning against the building. He nodded to the man, looked around, and not seeing the girls pushed his way inside.

The crowd was thick, but he elbowed his way to the edge of the dance floor, frowning as he saw Mary Frances dancing in the embrace of a blue-coated army lieutenant.

He had his quick, sharp pang of jealousy which always filled him at sight of Mary with another man. It was part of his own self-uncertainty that he would never be sure of her. He knew this vaguely and fresh anger rose to mingle with discontent left over from the argument in the carriage.

He turned, running directly into Sandy Bowers, and the little mine owner seized his arm. Bowers had two methods of greeting his guests. The women he conveyed quickly to his wife, the men he led into the bar.

Despite Vance Youngman's halfhearted protests he was pushed through the throng until they reached the shelter of the drinking place reserved for men.

Here some fifty had already gathered, men too old or shy for dancing. They clustered in small knots, their voices hoarse over the noise of the whining fiddles.

Bowers carved a path through to the bar, took a glass from one of the attendants and pressed it into Vance's hand.

"Cheers, boy." He raised his stemmed wineglass which had been empty for half an hour and pretended to drink.

Vance emptied his at a single gulp and Bowers handed it back to the bartender. "Take care of him, Mac." He turned away then, his duty done, leaving Vance to lean against the bar.

He finished his second drink, and then his third. Time lost its sharp meaning, and he had no real knowledge of how long he stood there, wrapped tightly in his bitter thoughts.

His attention came alive suddenly when through the haze of his abstraction he caught English's name.

He turned quickly, expecting to face Ken, but

instead found two army officers pressing forward.

One he recognized as the man who had been dancing with Mary Frances and he was about to speak when he realized that they were arguing. The shorter one held his companion's arm.

"Let's get a drink." His tone was almost pleading. "Don't let him spoil your evening, Crouse. This is the first party we've been to in months, and merely because that murderer English is here is no reason why you should leave."

Vance Youngman started.

"Did I hear you mention Ken English?"

The taller man had a jutting nose. He stared, his eyes a little bloodshot, his small mouth trembling.

"If he's a friend of yours, I have nothing to say." His voice was formal.

"He's no friend of mine." Youngman looked from one to the other, knowing he had drunk too much, that his head was not entirely clear. "Did I hear you call him a murderer?"

"You did," said Baker. It was obvious that he resented the interruption, and that he would have liked to lead his friend away, but Crouse shook off the restraining arm.

"Leave me alone. I warned English that I was going to tell everyone in the territory. Yes. He's a murderer. He killed my brother." He had visited the bar several times himself and all the emotion which had filled him that afternoon now broke the dam of his natural reticence. The violent words passed from him purging his soul of all the hate that festered there, and as he talked, some of the grim tightness faded from Youngman's face.

Fred Crouse's grief did not touch him. The stark agony in the man's eyes meant nothing to Youngman. He had but one thought. Here was a weapon against English, something that Mary Frances could not ignore. He could not wait to find her. He swung away, blundering against Max Crowford. Crowford tried to stop him, but Youngman jerked free and slipped through the press, seeking the girl and found her presently beside the main door.

"Where have you been?"

Mary Frances flushed. She had been enjoying herself thoroughly, but it piqued her that Vance should bring her to the party and then desert her.

"That's a question I might ask you if I couldn't smell the whiskey. You've been drinking again, and you promised . . ."

Vance brushed the reminder aside impatiently. "Wait until you hear what I have to tell you." His voice rose and several people turned to stare. "Wait until you hear that your friend English is a common murderer, and a cashiered army officer at that."

"Vance," Mary Frances caught his arm. She was very conscious of the interested crowd around them. "I'm sorry for the way I acted in the carriage." She added in a low voice, "Come and dance."

"I don't want to dance." He pulled free of her arm.

"Then come outside." She brushed past him, walking rapidly away toward the arbor without looking back.

For an instant he hesitated, then hurried after her, catching her just as she stepped inside the small slat structure.

"What's the idea of trying to run away?"

She swung to face him, all the humor in her dark eyes wiped out by rising anger. "I'm not running away, but if you must make a scene I prefer that you make it while we are alone. The rest of the people at this party can't be interested in what you have to say."

"Can't they now?" he smirked down at her, his good humor partly restored by the thought of what he would tell. "You can bet they would be. Everyone on Sun Mountain would be pleased to learn that the man who licked Sam Brown is no better than the man he whipped. He's a murderer, a turncoat, drummed out of the army."

Mary Frances stared at him. "I'm surprised that you don't have it published in the *Territorial Enterprise*. What is this absurd story?"

"It's no story." He was turning sullen again. "The man who told me is a younger brother of the officer English killed."

She gasped and he swept on. "English was mixed up with the sutler's daughter. He stole quartermaster supplies and sold them to the Indians, and killed his best friend to keep it quiet . . ."

"I don't believe it. I absolutely do not believe it."

". . . but he didn't get away with it." Vance was dogged. "The girl testified against him at the court-martial. What's the matter with you? What's this English to you? Are you in love with him?"

"That's a fine question for you to ask me." Hands on hips, she faced him, her eyes snapping. "Sometimes I do not know what to do with you. You act like a spoiled three-year-old."

"And how do you think you're acting?" All Youngman's anger had returned. He had the uncontrollable impulse to grasp her slender shoulders and shake her. As his hands came up, Mary Frances read his purpose in his eyes and took a quick step. But instead of backing away as he had expected, she came in close.

"Don't you dare touch me. I'll hit you right in the eye."

He fought for control, sucking in his breath sharply. "Ladies don't talk that way."

"And whoever told you I was a lady? Go back to South Carolina and find a girl who will blush and hide her eyes when you bawl her out. In the West we just don't act that way. We grow up perfectly able to take care of ourselves. Go ahead if you dare. Hit me."

He didn't hit her. He stood for an instant shaking from the intensity of his anger, then he swung around and left the arbor, and stalked toward the main hotel building.

"Well," said Mary Frances to no one in particular. "Well now, I never in the world." She sat down on the rude bench. She did not cry. Tears were the farthest thing from her mind. She cupped her small chin in her hand and moodily stared at Youngman's retreating back. She saw him reach the hotel doorway, saw him stop to speak to someone waiting there.

Chapter Fourteen

Vance Youngman's first impulse was to walk away in the darkness. Instead he decided on the bar. Damn her, he thought, she's always right. I'm always wrong. It would serve her well if I got drunk.

He reached the building to find Max Crowford's square-bulked body blocking the entrance, and tried to step around the man, but Crowford stopped him, one hand on his shoulder.

Crowford was not as tall as Terry, and lacked a good thirty pounds of the judge's solid weight, but he still towered well above Youngman. "Wait a minute. I want to talk to you."

Youngman was in no mood to talk to anyone, certainly not to Crowford whom he thoroughly disliked, but there was not room to pass through the door with Crowford standing there.

The man's face was almost square beneath the shelter of the uneven beard. High cheekbones and the powerful hinge of the heavy jaw stretched the cheek skin flat and taut. The nose had a high hook and his eyes as he turned them on Youngman were hot and compelling and a little malicious.

"You're not very smart."

Vance's smoldering anger broke into the open. He resented the power which Crowford at times exerted over Terry.

Crowford was Terry's oldest friend. He had come to California in the judge's party and had been associated with the leader of the Golden Circle for years.

Most of the members looked on him as an ignorant frontiersman, only a slight cut above Sam Brown and the other toughs. There were whispers of killings along the Rio Grande, of vicious cruelties against the Mexicans, and instinctively the fastidious Youngman despised the man.

But Crowford was not to be denied. He had no liking for Youngman, no patience with the hotheaded boy, but he was willing to use anyone to further his cause.

Unlike Terry, Max Crowford had no patriotic feeling for the South. Long ago he had seen this trouble coming and had grasped the opportunity to turn the crisis to his own ends. He had encouraged Terry to cross the mountains to the Comstock and had managed to make the judge the leader of the Golden Circle.

Taking the measure of the men with whom they were associated, he gauged their strengths and their weaknesses, and so made his plans.

When the time came he intended to head the army which would claim Sun Mountain, run out the lawful owners, and turn the properties over to his followers.

This then was Crowford's dream, greater than Walker's, as far reaching as Lopez's. A rich western state, its economy based on the sunny valleys of California, the lush forests of Oregon, the fabulous mines of western Utah, and with himself as military dictator.

Then he could treat with Jeff Davis and the South, trading them Washoe silver in return for their support of his free hand on the west coast. With this in mind he had recruited his army, enrolling Sam Brown and the other toughs, men who had no political interest in the coming fight, but ruffians who would battle solely in the hope of profit.

The more conservative leaders of the Circle objected to the presence of the hired killers, but Terry trusted Crowford, thought him a loyal man, without ambition of his own; and Doctor

McMeans held him in contempt, willing to use Crowford's strength and fighting ability, yet believing that in the end Crowford would not share in the leadership to which the doctor himself aspired.

Both fitted neatly into the careful pattern of Crowford's master plan. Terry was his front, the screen behind which he worked. Under his direction councils of the Golden Circle had been set up in every major town of Oregon and California. And these councils awaited only the word from Washoe to break into open rebellion.

But it was the Comstock which must be the key to Crowford's operation. Without the flood of silver which poured daily from the depths of Sun Mountain he knew that they could not hope for lasting success.

Therefore Crowford remained in Washoe, organizing the company of men he had recruited, importing powder and ball through John Everett's store, and readying himself for the day when the pony express would bring the news that the South had at last seceded.

Purposely he held himself under constant check, but some of his pressing impatience crowded up into his voice as he said to Youngman, "I tell you that you aren't smart. When you were talking to those army officers at the bar it never occurred to you to ask why English visited Fort Churchill."

English's name cut through Youngman's anger, and he said in a compressed voice, "What are you talking about?"

Crowford's contempt was undisguised. "All you could think of was the girl. You had to rush out, to tell her that English was a murderer. You didn't once wonder why a man who had been cashiered from the service should visit the fort."

Youngman turned sullen. "What of it?"

"Only this," said Crowford. "I took up the conversation where you left. Young Crouse was so full of hate that he did not guard his tongue. Baker couldn't shut him up. English is after our guns. He admitted to Stewart that he comes from Washington. He wants Stewart to confiscate them as army property."

Thoughtless as he was, Vance Youngman understood. "But we need those rifles, without them Burke's damn firemen would run us off the mountain, we'd better . . ."

"Never mind," said Crowford. "You weren't made to think. We're all right for the moment. Jasper Stewart refused to act. His orders don't cover such a move. But we know now that English did come out here from Washington. What we have to learn is whether he came alone, and what the new administration plans to do about western Utah."

Youngman wet his lips uncertainly. "I wish Terry was here."

"To hell with Terry. Go in and round up half a dozen Circle members. Don't let anyone know what you're about. This party is crawling with Burke's firemen. If they guess that we're after English we'll have a battle on our hands. I want to take him quietly."

"But where is he? I haven't seen him around."

Crowford smiled wickedly. "He just went into that arbor where your girl is. Before that he was leaning against the corner of the stable. I've been watching him for the last half-hour."

Youngman cursed under his breath and swung around, but Crowford grabbed his arm. "Stop it you fool. We'll take care of English. Don't worry about that. You go and round up some men. I'll watch here. I'm not going to let him get away."

Chapter Fifteen

Mary Frances was still watching Youngman when English appeared in the arch, the lantern behind him casting his long shadow the full length of the arbor, tall and erect and adult.

"You look almost as angry as Youngman does," he said, stooping a little so that his flat-crowned hat would clear the low top of the entrance.

"Get out of here. No, wait," she rose to her feet, facing him. "Where did you come from?"

His quick smile lighted the dark tanned face. "I went for a long ride today and coming back this evening I found a lady in distress. Her carriage had broken down, so, I gave her a hand and she insisted that I come to her party."

"Mrs. Bowers," she guessed.

"And a fine lady, even if she is rich."

Mary Frances had a long moment to study his face. "I most certainly didn't expect to see you in Carson again," her attack was direct, "after the way you slipped out of our house without saying good-bye."

"But I did, to your father." He was not disconcerted.

"Oh." She was suddenly angered by her stupidity. "I thought when Father came to talk to you that night he was up to something. What was it?"

"I haven't said it was anything."

She shook her head. "Mr. English, I thought I proved to you that when I set myself to find out something I always succeed. At first I feared that Terry had had you spirited away, then we heard you were safe on Sun Mountain. How did you persuade father to let you go, or did he persuade you?"

"Well . . ."

She considered thoughtfully. "He doesn't approve of our supposed friendship, was that it?"

"Well," Ken English had no intention of betraying John Everett's proposal, but he was no match for Mary Frances.

"So he offered money if you would leave without seeing me," she pressed him.

English was startled. "That's a wild guess . . ."

"It is not a wild guess." She had read confirmation in the shading of his tone. "I know my father. He has made a great deal of money and is impressed by it. How much did he give you? If you don't answer, I'll ask him. I'll tell him that you've already told me."

"You wouldn't do that."

"I most positively would. As a little girl I found that the way to make people tell me things was to pretend I already know all about it."

His smile was a little weak. "You must have been a very disagreeable child."

She dimpled. "I most certainly was, and I still am. Are you going to tell me, or do I ask Father?"

He said slowly, "I'd hate to have your father think that I broke my faith."

"So you did take his money, how much?"

English's laugh was wholehearted. "You beat anyone I've ever met. I didn't take the money; satisfied?"

"Not until you tell me how much he offered. I have a very particular reason for wanting to know."

"Well." English shrugged. "You've wormed most of the story out of me. I suppose you might as well know the rest. He said that the manager of his San Francisco store would pay me five thousand dollars if I left western Utah."

Her small mouth formed a round *O* of amazement. "Five thousand dollars? He must think you an extremely dangerous man if he is willing to pay that much, why, that's a fortune."

English nodded with mock gravity. "It most certainly is."

"But you haven't gone. You're still here. Senator Seward must be paying you highly for you to refuse such a sum."

"He's paying me nothing. I told you my trip was unofficial."

She studied him frankly, her head a little to one side. "I'm glad, I mean I'm glad you refused father's offer because if you had taken it I would never be certain that the rest of the things weren't true."

He stiffened a little. "What are you chattering about now?"

She said, "I never chatter. I am talking about those foul things which Vance heard from the army officers."

He was very still for a moment, then he said in a different tone, "So that's what you two were quarreling about?"

"Partly," she admitted. "And at the very first I wasn't quite sure, because you had run away without a word and a man who would do a rude thing like that might do anything."

He didn't speak, and after a moment she went on. "But now I know it isn't the truth, because Vance said you were a thief and a man who is a thief would have taken that money from my father."

"You're jumping at conclusions."

"I never jump at conclusions. And if the part about you being a thief is false, the rest is probably untrue, especially that part about the sutler's daughter. Was she very good-looking?"

"Like an imp of hell." The words were wrenched from him.

"And you loved her very much?"

He was thoroughly startled. "Loved her? I hated the ground she walked on. I still do."

"Well," she said, and her tone warmed with pleased satisfaction. "I think you'd better tell me all about it."

His tone was as near rudeness as she had ever heard it. "I don't care to talk about it."

She shook her head. "Now you are being foolish, and I'm not prying just because I'm curious, but sometimes a person gets so chock-full of things that it's better if they kind of get it out of their system. Are you ashamed to tell me?"

He passed a hand slowly over his eyes. Mike Lynch had been right. Nothing was ever finished. The years had not buried the tragedy. Fred Crouse had this day brought its sequence rushing back upon him.

He saw the court, the impassive faces of the officers. He heard again the pleading voice of the man assigned to represent him. "You've got to tell the truth," Herbert had begged. "You've got to tell them exactly what happened."

He hadn't told then, but he knew suddenly that he meant to tell this girl. He did not stop to analyze the reasons, he only knew that he wanted her to know, wanted her to hear the defence which he had never used.

His voice came colorless as he held himself under deep restraint, not daring to let his emotion touch his words.

He said, "It was a small post on the Arkansas, back country, and Paul Crouse was in command. He'd been my friend at school, and I'd spent my leaves at his family's home. I hadn't been assigned a week when I realized what this sutler's girl was doing to Paul. She'd changed him and I didn't like it, and then by chance I learned he was helping the sutler to steal quartermaster supplies to sell to the Indians."

He stopped for a moment as if to gather breath and Mary Frances said in a hushed voice, "But why would he . . . ?"

English's shoulders moved tiredly. "Who knows? The girl had a stranglehold on him and Paul was weak. That's the part I couldn't understand, that he was weak." The steady words broke for a moment then went on.

"I had a talk with the girl. I tried to reason with her but she laughed at me. I lost my temper and threatened her. Of course she went to Paul.

"We . . . we had a row and I knocked him down. I had a temper in those days. I . . . I handle it better now, but the damage was done. He could have had me tried. Instead he challenged me. The dueling pistols were hair-triggered, and I wasn't used to them. I meant to shoot over his head. I killed him by accident."

She was silent, feeling the depth of his grief, knowing that what he said was true, and then she said softly, "So you took the blame for Paul's theft, you didn't even defend yourself at your court-martial, did you?"

He moved his hands outward, almost in a pleading gesture. "Paul's family had treated me like their own son. His death hurt them enough."

She shook her head vigorously. "Oh, but you're wrong. With Paul dead they needed to believe in you. As it is they lost two sons. Did you say that you did the stealing?"

He was startled, then he said wryly, "I didn't have to. The sutler was already caught. By implicating me he earned a lighter sentence. His daughter hated me for killing Paul. She did the best she could to have me hanged."

Mary Frances looked at him shrewdly. "And sometimes you wish that you had."

He nodded, his mouth bitter.

"Now," she said, "you're feeling sorry for yourself, and that isn't good. I'm wondering after what has happened that you went near Fort Churchill. You couldn't have known that Lieutenant Crouse was there."

"I didn't," he admitted. "I had to see Captain Stewart."

"And why," said Max Crowford, "did you have to see Captain Stewart?" He had crossed the yard silently and now stood behind English, his heavy gun in his hand.

"No, don't turn. Don't try to reach that revolver."

English was frozen. Mary Frances made no sound. The back of her small hand was pressed tightly across her mouth. Her eyes dilated until they looked twice natural size.

For a full minute there was no movement in the shadows of the arbor. Then English said in a steady, emotionless voice, "What's this, Crowford?"

Max Crowford laughed, a heavy chuckle without the lightening of mirth. "It's the end of the road, English. No, don't move yet. I've got half a dozen men with me, and we want to talk to you."

"Talk then," said English.

"Not here. They're bringing horses along the back road. We'll pick a place to talk where it will be quieter. Keep your hands up, and walk out of there backwards unless you want a bullet in the spine."

English saw horror grow in Mary Frances' eyes. He saw them change, crystallize with purpose, and knew suddenly that she intended something and was afraid for her.

He took a step backwards, not because of Crowford's threat, but because of the girl, because he did not want her involved in this.

A second step carried him through the opening into the yard, but he counted without Mary Frances.

She came forward in a little rush, using both hands to lift the gun from his belt, her motion partly screened by English's big body. Had it been a double-action she might have succeeded, but her thumbs lacked the strength to pull back the hammer and the fumbling second she used to try gave Crowford time.

He jumped in, knocking English aside with his lumpy shoulder and twisted the girl, wrenching the gun from her grasp.

English lost his balance and fell against the arbor, the lathes shattering under his weight. He tried to struggle upward to close with Crowford, and four men smothered him as he rose.

For an instant he was like a wild bull, throwing one aside, ripping free of the second, then the barrel of a gun crashed down on his hat crown and he fell forward onto his knees.

He stayed there for a full moment, the ground under his big hands spinning. In that moment he heard Crowford's harsh voice. "Youngman, take care of this wildcat. She's your woman. Hang on to her before I break her head."

There was a swirl of angry skirts and Mary

Frances saying in savage fury, "You take your hands off me, Vance Youngman. If you don't let me go this instant you'll be sorry, you'll be positively sorry to the last day you live."

English did not hear Youngman's answering grunt. Two men reached down, seizing his arms, and hoisted English to his feet, a third got the knife from his boot top.

Crowford was saying, "Move him out, get him into those trees. We don't want Burke's crowd to see us. Step on it."

One of the men who held English growled, "What about the girl? The little hellcat will raise the alarm."

Crowford glared at Mary Frances. It was obvious from his expression that he would like to throttle her. Youngman stood behind her, holding her arms locked at her sides with both of his.

"It looks," said Crowford sourly, "as if you've lost a girl, Vance. It looks as if English was too much for you."

Vance Youngman snarled something which none of them could hear. Mary Frances paid him not the slighest attention. Her eyes were on English.

"Are you hurt, are you all right?"

He managed to nod. His head was still spinning a little from the blow, beginning to ache.

"Don't worry," she said, and then to Crowford, "When I get through telling Judge Terry what you've done, he'll run you absolutely out of the territory."

"Will he?" said Crawford, without much interest. "Take her over to the stable, Vance. Keep her there until we've gone. After that, I don't care what you do with her. I know what I'd do in your shoes, but you won't, you're too damn much of a gentleman."

Mary Frances stared at him for a moment, and then without warning she kicked Vance Youngman on the knee cap. He let out a yell and dropping the girl's arms danced about on one leg.

Mary Frances started to run. She never had a chance. Max Crawford grabbed her arms as she tried to dash past him, swung her around and abruptly clipped her on the jaw with his free hand.

As she collapsed toward the ground Ken English went crazy. He jerked free of the men who held him, diving at Crowford, his clawing fingers locking about the big man's throat.

Someone swung up a gun and pounded it down on his head. He had to strike three times before English's fingers dropped free and he fell heavily to the ground, not moving.

Chapter Sixteen

Sam Brown's station on the river was half of logs, half mud, a ramshackle building, as slovenly and repelling as its owner.

No one in the territory who knew Brown stopped there from choice unless he was numbered among the non-descript drifters who made up Sam's clan of thieves and cutthroats.

Chance travelers attracted by the lights and the need of rest sometimes paused, and regretted it, lucky to escape without their purses, without their horses.

Some had not escaped; more than one nameless way-farer was buried in the soft ground behind the station where the river encroached on the sandy soil.

Inside the one large room a rusty stove

warmed the far corner, a single plank, resting on two kegs made do for a bar, and a half-dozen battered tin cups furnished drinking equipment. A sack of flour sagged beside the battered stove, and hams and bacon hung like a lumpy canopy from the smoked rafters overhead.

The dirty floor was the only sleeping place and the air was fouled with a mixture of wood smoke, tobacco smoke, old cooking smells, stale whiskey odors, and the acrid tang of human sweat.

It was into this dismal place that Ken English was half led, half dragged by Crowford's men.

Brown, sitting beside the open oven door, his sock feet resting on it and a half tin cup of whiskey in his hands, watched incuriously as Crowford came through the door. He made no move to rise until he saw English, then he leaped to his feet.

"Well damn my eyes." His red whiskers were not now tied under his chin but hung down straggly and uncombed over the neckband of his dirty shirt.

He stood flat-footed, still, watching them fumble English onto the bench beside the rude table, then his eyes shifted to Crowford.

"What goes on? What are you doing with him?" He pointed a stub thumb at the dazed prisoner.

Crowford walked around him toward the

stove and warmed his hands, rubbing out the night chill which had turned his fingers stiff.

"A spy for Lincoln," he said, shortly. "We're going to ask him some questions, and we didn't want to be disturbed."

Sam Brown's red-rimmed eyes studied English's slumped figure. Ken's hat was gone, his hair matted with dry blood. "Looks like he didn't want to come."

Crowford shrugged. "How about some whiskey, Sam? It's bone-chill outside since the wind came up."

"Help yourself." Sam waved his hand toward the whiskey barrel, never taking his hungry eyes from English. "A man who serves himself don't get short-measured."

Max Crowford laughed. "You're a damn lazy bum," he said in unaccustomed good humor. "Why in hell don't you clean out this mare's-nest?"

Brown looked around in genuine surprise. He was almost sober, and not quarrelsome, as usual. Besides, he always showed Crowford a healthy respect which he wasted on few men.

"Clean it? Why, it's clean enough. What's the matter with it?"

"Never mind," said Crowford. He walked to the make-shift bar, selected a cup, and wiping it somewhat cleaner with a bit of rag, broached the keg.

His action brought his companions forward crowding around him, waiting their turn.

Sam Brown gave them no heed. His eyes again fixed with animal intensity on the motionless English. His only movement was his hand which fondled the haft of the big knife.

His mouth hung parted, showing stained teeth through the break in the unruly beard, and he breathed through it, rather than through his heavy nose.

But the breathing made no more sound than the panting of an anxious dog. "Want me to make him talk?"

Max Crowford shrugged away from the bar. "You can help," he said, in tolerant amusement. He glanced at English, very pleased with the night's work. "Let him alone for a while. Robbins beat him over the head until his brains are scrambled. I want him to know what we're talking about when I start to question him."

He eased down onto the other end of the rough bench and worked off one of his boots, straightening a wrinkle in his sock.

"The damn thing's killing me," he remarked to no one in particular, and pulled the boot back into place. "What about something to eat, Sam? We had to leave old Bowers' party before any of us got a chance at the grub."

Brown jerked a thumb toward the smoked meat hanging above their heads. "Wouldn't hurt to fry up a mess of fatback. Skillet's on the stove."

A man at the bar spoke without turning. "That's what I like about Sam's hotel. You always get such fancy service."

Sam glared at the speaker. Crowford paid no attention. He stepped onto the bench, then to the table top, reaching down a moldy side of pork. He fumbled in his pockets, then looked at Brown.

"Let me have your knife, Sam."

Brown drew the sixteen-inch blade, standing for a moment, caressing the bright steel, running the calloused ball of his thumb along the razor edge, then slowly he shook his head so that the uneven ends of his scraggly whiskers whipped a little.

"Sorry, Max, but I don't like to go dulling my knife on any lousy bacon. I keep it for more tender meat." His eyes went back to English, warmed by an inner pleasure of anticipation.

Crowford laughed again. "Hell," he said, and there was a hint of grudging admiration in his tone, "you're more wolf than man. Just don't start whittling until I give the word."

Beside him a man shuddered. "I don't like any of this." There was protest in his tone. "Crowford, it's not human to use a knife on a man. If you have to shoot, yes, or even a rope, but to use a knife, like a butcher . . ."

"That's Sam." Crowford had borrowed a knife from one of the others and cut away the moldy rind. "A butcher who loves his work." His eyes hardened as they lifted to the man. "This isn't a game, Martin. It's war, and English is a spy."

Martin growled in offended anger, "I can fight as well as the next, but Brown isn't human, He's a ghoul."

"I'm what?" Brown turned his shaggy head. "I'm a chief."

"That's what he means, Sam," Crowford said hastily, wanting no trouble among his followers.

"Oh!" Sam relaxed, pleased. "He don't know how big a chief I am. Did he ever hear about the time I killed a man and they laid him out on a pool table, back of Ryan's? Blood dripped down, but that didn't bother me. I crawled under that table and went plumb to sleep. Didn't bother me. Nothing bothers me. I just ain't got nerves, you might say."

Crowford did not answer. He had the slab of meat trimmed, and walking to the stove pulled the blackened pan forward over the fire and began to slice the meat into it. The conversation lagged as they listened to it sizzle.

Ken English heard the sizzle. He had been hearing the mutter of conversation without paying accurate attention. His head hurt, his eyes felt hot and feverish and he had a gnawing nausea at the pit of his stomach.

He knew that he was groggy, but he was not too far gone to understand some of the movement around him. He had heard Crowford tell Brown that he was a spy and that they had brought him here for questioning.

He knew what that meant, but his perceptions were so dulled by the blows which had battered him to the ground that he sat considering the fear he should be experiencing, and wondered vaguely why he was not afraid.

They were eating now, with appetites sharpened by the night's ride. Only Brown refused the food. He still stood between English and the stove, and Ken, opening his eyes and looking up, met Brown's steady stare.

He heard Brown's rumble. "I think he's coming out of it. Shall I start on him, Max?"

"Not yet," said Crowford. "Give him a slug of coffee, Martin. Might put some whiskey in it."

Martin brought the cup. His ministrations had little of compassion, yet he was not too rough. He put the handle into English's grasp and helped him raise it to his mouth. The hot, black liquid coursed down through him, making him conscious of his body. Until that moment his head had felt as if it were floating freely in the smoky room.

"Feeling better?"

English was. The whiskey in the drink stimulated his sluggish circulation. He looked around slowly and then took another sip.

"Thanks," he muttered. His eyes went away from Brown to center on Crowford, and a recurring emotion came to fill him. It was hate.

His mind was still too foggy to analyze this new absorption, to connect it with Crowford's striking down the girl. He only knew, sitting there, that he hated Crowford as he had never hated anyone in his life.

Until this moment his reactions toward the members of the Golden Circle had been detached, not personalized. But this was very personal and he tried to understand exactly why he should experience it.

Crowford had been watching the effect of the coffee. He said, "Try a little more whiskey," and Martin moved back toward the barrel.

"How you feeling, English?"

Ken shook his head slowly. It was a thorough effort to talk. "All right." The answer was purely instinctive, an unwillingness to admit hurt before these men.

Crowford laughed. "You take a lot of punishment, but it isn't a patch to what you can expect if you don't give us some straight answers. So Lincoln sent you to Washoe? Why?"

Ken thought this over painfully. "It wasn't Lincoln."

"Who then?"

He shook his head. "I don't remember."

"I'll make him remember." Sam Brown took a half-step forward, the knife eagerly poised.

Crowford put up a hand. "I said to wait."

Brown stopped, grumbling. Crowford got up and walked around to stand in front of English. "You aren't buying yourself a thing by acting stubborn," he warned. "We already know that you've been to the Fort, that you tried to get Jasper Stewart to take our guns."

That was it, that was what English had been trying to remember. His slow thoughts now grouped things into an ordered sequence. He'd gone to the fort to get the guns, and then he'd gone to a party, and Fred Crouse was there. Fred Crouse had talked, he'd talked to Vance Youngman, and Youngman had told the girl. His eyes went slowly around the room. Every man in it had his full attention centered on English.

But Youngman wasn't there.

The knowledge worried him in some obscure way. It was something intangible, something he could not quite grasp. Where was Youngman? What had happened to Mary Frances? He had the memory of Crowford knocking her down, of her lying motionless before the little arbor, of jumping at Crowford, and then nothing.

"Answer me," said Crowford.

Answer him what? Oh, about the guns. The guns didn't seem of importance. Why had he been worrying about the guns, what did they have to do with him, with Mary Frances? Why should Crowford worry about them?

He put a hand on the bench at his side and tried to lift himself to his feet. Mary Frances. He had to get out of here, he had to find out what had happened to the girl.

Crowford knocked him down. It was a shove rather than a blow, but he was so unsteady that he went flat onto the dirty floor. He lay quiet, his cheek pressed against the grit on the scuffed boards, feeling as if he would never manage to get up again.

He had help. Two men seized him, lifting him by the shoulders. Crowford said, "You're being stupid, English. You haven't got a chance in the world. You can make it simpler if you talk."

There was grit mixed with the blood on his lips. He tried to spit it away. He mumbled, "What's there to say? You know about the rifles."

"You didn't come here alone." Crowford was shaking him. "Those slave lovers in Washington wouldn't send one man by himself. Who are you working with? Who came with you?"

English managed to say, "Nobody."

"Look," said Crowford. "I'm a patient man. I'm a man who never goes rushing at things, but I also mean what I say. I want to know Lincoln's plans. I want to know what they mean to do about the west coast. Will they send more troops here when the war starts, or will they pull the defenses out of the territory?"

English shook his head slowly. He didn't know. He tried to tell them that he didn't know. He heard Crowford curse. He heard Sam Brown say, "I can make him talk. Just let me at him, Max. He'll love to talk when I cut his gizzard out."

"Try his thumbs," said Crowford. "Swing him up to that meat hook. Give him another shot of whiskey first. I don't want him passing out before I'm ready."

They poured a full fiery cup down his throat. It knocked some of the haze from behind his eyes. For a moment he was clearheaded, he knew exactly what was happening, and then the stuff hit him like the jolt of a kicking mule.

He was drunk. He knew he was drunk. He wanted to howl. He wanted to leap up and hurl the table at Crowford's head. He had never been a heavy drinker, but the alcohol on his empty stomach coupled with the beating he had received acted as a powerful stimulant.

They grabbed his arms and somewhere he found the strength to throw them aside. He heaved the table over and grabbing the bench tried to swing it.

Sam Brown was stalking toward him and he threw the bench at the man's knees. Brown jumped back to escape it and Crowford chose that instant to land on English's back.

Ken tried to throw the man over his head, but Crowford's weight carried them both to the floor.

The crowd came to Crowford's aid, their very number almost defeating their purpose, and all the time Crowford was shouting in his hoarse voice.

"Don't kill him. Don't kill him until I can question him."

It struck English as funny. He wanted to laugh. They weren't to kill him, not yet. They had him down, face to the floor, spread-eagled, one man holding each of his arms, one on each leg. He couldn't move. He could hardly breathe, and yet he wanted to howl with laughter.

They pulled him upright again. They were looping cords about his thumbs. The cords were jerked tight, forcing his arms above his head, forcing him onto tiptoe, lifting him until the front edge of his boot soles barely grazed the rough floor.

Involuntarily he cried out with the pain. The sinews of his arms were pulled tight. His thumbs felt as if they would tear loose from their sockets. The pain drove the alcohol haze from his mind.

Crowford rasped the table around and sat down upon it. He was breathing heavily, his chest rising and falling sharply under his shirt.

"Now," he said, "let's get down to business.

Who sent you to Washoe? Lincoln?"

"Seward," said English. He saw no harm in their knowing. They knew so much already. The pain was getting worse in his arms, but his thumbs were turning numb.

"Seward, huh?" Crowford considered the answer, turning it over in his mind. "And you were supposed to get our guns?"

English moved his head in what might have been a nod. He saw no reason for not answering that either. Crouse had already told them about the guns.

"Fine," said Crowford. "Keep talking. The more you talk the quicker we'll cut you down."

"That's all." English's mind was clouding again. He fought to clear it without too much success. His vision blurred, but he could still see Crowford's face. He thought that he would probably always see it. His one emotion now was hate, hate burning through him.

"That's all," he managed through lips so stiff that he could hardly move them.

Crowford slapped him across the face, using his riding gloves, the leather turned rough and harsh from contact with the wet.

The stinging force of the blow jarred English's swaying consciousness. "Who are you working with? Burke?"

He shook his head.

Crowford hit him again. "Who else? How

many men has Burke got?"

Again Crowford hit him. English surprised himself by saying in a high thin voice, "You'd better kill me while you can. You'd better kill me."

It was the last word he uttered before he lapsed into unconsciousness.

Chapter Seventeen

Mary Frances Everett could not remember ever being quite so angry in her life. She roused to find her sister bending over her, to see Mrs. Bowers with a smelling-salts bottle in her hand, to be aware of other women standing about the small room, staring at her.

Ruth was crying, and Mary Frances' first really conscious thought was that tears were the only way her sister ever greeted an emergency.

Someone had loosened her clothes, and she sat up bringing one hand to her small jaw, finding the lump already forming there. The lump was what roused her anger, and the memory of Crowford's blow. Yet her rage was directed not so much at Max Crowford as it was at Youngman.

"Where's Vance?"

Ruth stared at her as if she were a ghost suddenly risen. "Please, lie still . . . you'll . . ."

"Stuff and nonsense," Mary Frances told her. "And stop that sniffling." She looked about at the staring women, then reached out her hand to Mrs. Bowers for the smelling-salts bottle and took a healthy sniff.

It almost knocked the top of her head off, but it did bring her to her feet. She took time to arrange her clothes and hair, to smile her thanks to the women.

"Excuse me," she said to no one in particular, and stalked out of the room.

Everyone in the main hotel room stared at her. She knew a moment's embarrassment, but that was driven from her mind as her eyes found Vance Youngman.

"You . . ." she said, "you . . ." and headed toward him, people between moving hastily out of her way.

Vance wet his lips nervously. "Mary Frances, listen . . ."

"I," she said, "will do the talking. You are the one who should do the listening, and don't you forget it." She felt Ruth at her elbow and turned impatiently to her. "You go get our wraps, and stop crying."

Then she swept out into the yard and after a moment's hesitation Vance trailed after her.

"Mary Frances, please . . ."

"You," she said, "are a worm. You are so far beneath contempt that I can't find words to fit you. What have Max Crowford and his crowd of cutthroats done with Ken English?"

Vance Youngman spoke between desperation and anger. "The man is a spy. He . . ."

"And you," she cut in, "go around watching your friends knock down girls, and listening to lies about decent people. I don't want ever to see you again, and even that would be too soon."

He started at her, his young face settling into bitter, pouting lines. "If that's the way you feel . . ."

"That's absolutely, utterly the way I feel. If I had a gun I'd take the greatest pleasure in blowing your head into pieces."

Ruth flurried through the door, her face still showing the stain of her crying. She handed Mary Frances her cape and looked haughtily over Vance Youngman's head.

Mary Frances strode toward the stable with Youngman at her heels, plainly at a loss what to do. At last he offered, "I'll drive you home."

"You most certainly will not."

"I . . . well, at least I'll hitch the team for you."

"That," said Mary Frances distantly, "is not at all necessary. I am entirely capable of hitching them up myself. Come on, Ruth."

Youngman stared after them, black rage welling up to fill his soul. He was angry with the girl, but most of his rage centered on English. Since the man's arrival he had had nothing but trouble. It did not occur to him that a great deal of his difficulties could be traced to his own actions. He only knew that English offered a real threat, both to the plans for taking the lode, and to his own personal future.

He flung around and crowding back into the house, ignoring the questioning stares of those he passed, made his way to the bar.

Mary Frances never once looked back. Holding Ruth's arm she piloted the older girl across the hard-packed yard toward the stable. The team which Vance had rented stood harnessed, tethered to the rear of the carriage, and Mary Frances set about hitching them vigorously, ignoring the damage which the operation wrought to her dress. She had almost finished when a tall man stepped through the shadows.

"Can I help you, ma'am?"

She spun on him, thinking it was Vance, and found that she was facing a stranger, and said levelly, "And who might you think you are?"

The man smiled. "I don't think much about it, ma'am, but they call me Tom Burke."

Mary Frances' mouth opened slowly. No sound came, and she closed it.

Burke stepped forward and catching the horses' bridles, backed the team expertly into place, then hooked up the leather traces. "Yes," he said to her unspoken question, "I'm *the* Tom Burke."

Ruth uttered a low moan. Her only experience with Tom Burke's firemen had been in her own kitchen, and she was now morally certain that she and Mary Frances were about to be murdered. If her sister shared the fear she gave no sign.

"And what are you doing here?"

Burke finished with the team and handed her the lines. "I wanted to talk to you," he said, offering his hand.

After a moment's hesitation she took it, allowing him to assist her into the carriage.

Ruth watched the action, standing as one paralyzed. She ignored Burke's offer of help and Mary Frances said with ready impatience, "Get in, Ruthie. If you stand there much longer you'll grow roots."

Ruth got in. Not until she was settled did the younger girl turn back to Burke. "Well, if you have something to say I think you'd better say it."

He nodded. "I couldn't help overhearing what is being said in the hotel, that Crowford carried off a man named English, and knocked you out in the bargain."

"And where were you when all this happened?"

He smiled slowly. "I just got here a few minutes ago, worse luck."

She considered him, recalling everything she had heard about him since arriving at Carson. From her father, from Youngman, from Terry's men she had gained a picture of a saloon rouster, a man who fought for the love of fighting, a man who was feared if not respected by the Southern party.

Her eyes studied his face, finding it weathered, wrinkled, even scarred, for there was an old knife wound across one cheek. But his eyes were steady and open and unflinching under her gaze.

She said a little waspishly, "If you are a friend of Mr. English I think you should arrange it better than to allow him to come to a place like this alone."

His lips then held a faint trace of a smile. He was a man who could be hard and stern in dealing with men, but there was a natural courtesy in him that would not allow him to be rude to a woman, any woman.

"I'm not a particular friend of Ken English," he told her. "We've met once, and at that meeting I found him stubborn and unco-operative. I haven't talked to him since."

"Then why . . . ?"

"Why am I here?" He studied her face for a moment. "Because he and I are trying to accomplish the same thing. But aside from that, I am not a friend of Terry's men or anything that they stand for."

The words reminded her that her father was a friend of Terry, that her father was opposed to Burke and that out of family loyalty she should be against this man.

But her worry about Ken English was more deep-seated than her loyalty to her father. She did not stop to analyze this, to consider either her feelings or her attitude.

She said, "What is it that you want from me?"

"Where did Crowford take English?"

She shook her head slowly. "He didn't say. He said that he wanted to talk to him where they wouldn't be disturbed."

"Did he take him back to Virginia?"

"He probably did, to one of Terry's forts."

They looked at each other in strained silence. "What do you think they mean to do with him after they finish their questions?"

She said steadily, "I think they mean to kill him." At her side she heard Ruth's strangled gasp. She wanted to gasp herself. Until that moment she had not even allowed herself to think about it.

Burke nodded slowly. "I'm afraid you're right. What about Vance Youngman? Would he know where they've taken English?"

"He wouldn't tell," said Mary Frances.

"He could be made to." Burke was already turning away.

Her mind was in tumult. She tried to order her thoughts and failed. She didn't want Vance hurt, and yet when she considered Ken English she experienced a slow, dull feeling of despair.

"I . . . please . . ." But Burke was striding back toward the hotel.

He didn't look around. He heard the carriage start, heard the horses' hoofs on the hard ground. He thought, Things are never simple, at least in a situation of this kind. Loyalties are not clear. People are divided by their purposes and aims.

He was not worrying about Ken English. To him English was little more than a pawn in a game, but the very fact Crowford had dared seize him from the midst of Sandy Bowers' party filled Tom Burke with uneasiness.

Tomorrow the Southern wing would be crowing on the mountain that they had bested Tom Burke. And in a time when the balance of power hung by the slenderest thread, he could not permit his enemies a victory of any kind.

Feeling thus he entered the hotel, located a dozen of his firemen in the crowd, and motioned silently for them to follow him.

Vance Youngman was at the bar, leaning forward on his elbows, a glass between his hands, staring down at it moodily.

He did not look up at Burke's entrance. With his back turned to the door he remained unconscious of the fireman's arrival.

Burke looked over the room carefully. He had no desire to precipitate a fight. He knew Sandy Bowers well and liked him, and he knew that Sandy would resent any move that started a roughhouse at the party. He wanted to get Youngman outside as quietly as possible.

He left his men clustered in the door and walked toward the bar, passing Fred Crouse standing dark and sullen and angry, and Lieutenant Baker trying to get his companion to go home.

Burke considered them with a general's caution and decided that they would take no part in this. There were some twelve or fifteen others in the room besides the bartenders, and he considered them also. Most he knew at least slightly, and he saw not one of Terry's known followers among them.

They too, he thought, would stay out.

Satisfied then, he went on to stand at Youngman's elbow, saying in a calm, level voice, "You're wanted outside, Vance."

Youngman turned slowly. He had been so bemused by his own bitterness that for a full instant he did not seem to recognize Burke. When he did, anger came up into his eyes, turning them stubborn and sultry and a little wild.

"Hell with you," he said. He came around and there was sudden violence in the set of his shoulders. His hand holding the glass swept up as if to fling the whiskey into Burke's face.

But Burke was too old a party in barroom brawls to be caught off guard. His right hand came down striking Youngman's wrist, knocking the glass from the boy's grasp. His left crossed in a sharp chopping blow which thudded brittly against the point of Youngman's jaw. The boy swayed, and Burke caught him before he could fall.

His strength was sufficient to hold the boy upright by one arm, although Youngman's eyes had glazed, his knees gone wobbly.

Fred Crouse saw the blow. He came forward a full step and said, "Here, what's going on?"

"Keep out of this," Burke told him, and used his free hand to push Crouse back into Baker's arms.

Others in the room turned, but before any one of them could move, Burke's firemen had surrounded him, and making a solid phalanx bore him and his captive through the uncertain crowd and out into the yard.

The night wind which had risen to cut

through the balmy air of the early evening swept off the rocky hills and struck Vance Youngman harshly in the face.

He had not been entirely out, and he shook his head in an effort to clear the daze, stumbling as the men pushed him ahead of them.

Sandy Bowers came from the hotel, calling Burke's name sharply, and Tom Burke shoved his prisoner into another's grasp saying, "Take him to the stables. I'll handle this."

He turned back then to face the mine owner. Others had crowded through the door behind Bowers and were staring curiously.

Burke returned to Bowers, saying in a low voice, "Go back inside, Sandy. It's none of your affair."

Bowers still held his empty champagne glass. He threw it onto the ground between them, to shatter with a tinkling sound.

"Dammit, Tom. I don't take kindly to trouble at my party."

"I didn't start it." Burke was reasonable. "Remember that, Sandy. I didn't start it."

Bowers considered him. He was not nearly as tall as Burke and he was forced to look up into the fireman's face.

"Let him go. I don't give a continental who started it. I won't have you taking a man out of my party."

"You can't stop us." Burke was still trying to

keep his voice reasonable. "You'll save trouble, Sandy, to go back inside and take your guests with you. You can't stop us."

"Someone can." It was Crouse. "I don't like to be shoved around, mister."

"Then keep out of my way," said Burke, his voice tightening suddenly. It was one thing to be reasonable in the face of Sandy Bowers, quite another in the face of these junior officers. He was still smarting under the treatment he had received when he had first asked Captain Stewart to interfere in the affairs on Sun Mountain.

Crouse's face flushed in anger, but Baker had his shoulder. "Easy, Fred, we don't know what this is all about."

"And you'll be wise not to find out," said Burke, and stalked toward the stables, not once looking back.

In the shadow of the adobe buildings his men were waiting, holding Youngman in their midst.

The boy stood sullenly between his captors, but at the sight of Burke he roused and began to swear in a low, deadly monotone.

"You're brave," he sneered. "A dozen men to jump one. If I had a gun you'd never have taken me. If I was free I'd beat you to death with my fists."

"Let him go," said Burke. He pulled his own gun from his belt and handed it to one of his companions. "If he licks me let him go."

For an instant after they freed him Youngman stood glaring around. Then he charged, his arms flailing like an uncontrolled windmill.

Tom Burke knocked him down. The fireman showed no more emotion than he would have at felling a tree with a sharp axe. He didn't use his boots on the fallen boy, nor did he make any effort to follow up his advantage. He just stood there, waiting for Youngman to rise from the hard trodden earth.

Youngman got slowly to his knees. He stayed there for a long moment as if not certain exactly what to do. Then he rose laboriously, stepping back as he did so.

A smear of blood blotted the corner of his mouth and he wiped this away with the back of his hand, his eyes sullenly intent on Tom Burke's face.

"You're too big." He said this almost grudgingly, as if the words were forced out of him. "If I had a gun . . . a gun evens things."

Tom Burke did not trouble to veil the contempt growing in his eyes. He reached for his gun, thrust it into the waistband of his pants, and said to a man on Youngman's right, "Give him yours, Hal."

The man grunted and handed Youngman the heavy gun, extending it barrel first so that Youngman must reverse the weapon before he could use it.

Vance Youngman's eyes had widened at Burke's words. He grasped the revolver eagerly, shooting a quick glance at Burke to see that the fireman's weapon was still safely under his belt. His hand jerked a little as if he meant to flip the gun in the air and catch it by the stock.

But the intent died swiftly, and the light which had leaped into his eyes as he met Burke's glance faded back. They stood thus for a full minute of heavy silence, neither moving, the fireman waiting, Youngman trying to bring himself to the point of trusting his luck.

Instead he began to shake. It was something beyond his control. It was the cracking of some inner fiber not resilient enough to stand the strain.

His gun dropped from nerveless fingers, bounced dully on the ground at his feet. No one moved as he suddenly buried his face in his hands, and dry sobs wracked his slender body.

Two or three of the men cleared their throats in embarrassment, then Burke said quietly, "Pick up your gun, Hal. Mr. Youngman won't be needing it now."

The man scooped it up, stared at it for a moment as if he had never seen it before, then wiped off the dirt on his sleeve and stuffed it back under his belt.

Vance Youngman choked with a sudden flaming rage, a shameful rage against himself. Always he had had secret doubts about himself, but always before there had been some excuse. He had even stood up against Sam Brown on the night when English had come to his rescue.

That was the high point. He had stood up, he knew now, because there had been no avoiding the issue once he had spoken. But facing Burke he had had a knowledge, a haunting sense that Burke would not kill him unless he made the first move.

And he had failed to make that move. He almost wished the gun was again in his hand, that he had the choice to make anew, and then he shuddered, aware that he would act the same way a second time. Facing Tom Burke was like facing an immovable mountain. The man lacked Brown's inherent cruelty, but he was entirely without personal fear, without nerves, as unstoppable as an avalanche.

Burke stepped forward until only a few feet separated him from the prisoner. "I'm going to ask you a question," he said in a toneless voice. "Don't lie to me. Do you know where they've taken English?"

"Where you'll never find him." Youngman tried his old bluster, but even in his own ears it sounded hollow and unconvincing.

Burke's eyes measured him shrewdly. "That means you don't know. You have no more idea than I have."

Youngman hadn't. He suspected that English had been taken to one of the forts, but he did not know this for sure, and it surprised him and added to his uncertainty to have Burke guess.

He said sullenly, "If you already know about it, why waste time questioning me?"

"Why indeed?" Tom Burke was talking half to himself, then his voice hardened. "I don't like you, Vance. I'm not threatening you. I'm just telling you. You're going to get on a horse tonight and you're going to ride out of the country, and you're not coming back. If you do, if I meet you any place in western Utah again, I'll kill you on sight."

Youngman stared at him angrily, but in spite of his conscious effort his eyes fell away first. He knew in that moment that he was completely beaten, that if he tried to stay on Sun Mountain he would be afraid to walk the streets for fear of meeting Burke.

He knew also that the tale of what had happened tonight would get around. He said dully, "I haven't got a horse."

"Give him one," said Burke.

A man disappeared into the stable, coming out leading a horse. No one said anything. Youngman walked over, pretended to examine the cinches. Then he swung up.

A moment later he spurred about and clattered out onto the hardness of the back road. A high, wild yell swept back to them, part anger, part defiance, part self-pity. It was the last that any of them ever saw of Vance Youngman.

Chapter Eighteen

Mary Frances Everett wheeled the rented team into her father's yard, flipped the reins around the whip and climbing down, marched toward the house.

Ruth was forced into a half-run to keep pace with her younger sister, and she cried breathlessly as they reached the kitchen door, "Mary, be careful what you do."

Mary Frances did not answer. Still at her high pace she went through the kitchen and broke unceremoniously in upon her father, working at his desk.

John Everett looked up fleetingly, then his eyes went back to the column of figures he had been adding.

"Home already? Didn't Vance come in with you?"

"Vance," said Mary Frances distinctly, "will not be coming to this house again."

Her father sighed. "Come, come. Have you two had another quarrel?"

"This is a great deal more than a quarrel," she said angrily. "You forget those silly figures of yours for a minute and listen to me."

John Everett put down his quill with the air of a long-suffering man whose patience had been extended almost to the breaking point. He turned and rose tiredly, his head coming only a little higher than his daughter's.

"Well now, what's your trouble?"

"You've got to ride to Virginia at once," she told him. "You've got to find Judge Terry and make him stop it."

"Stop what? What are you talking about?"

"I'm talking about the positively foul thing that Max Crowford and those toughs are doing to Ken English." Her voice rose until it was nearly a wail. "They're going to murder him. They will murder him if you don't stop them, and maybe even now it's too late."

John Everett's mouth opened slowly, then closed. He was staring at her face, taking in her swollen jaw.

"Maybe you'd better tell me what happened." His voice took on the dry, curt tone which he always used in talking business.

She told him then, the words coming in little breathless rushes, and as he listened his face changed, setting in harder lines, seeming to age.

When she finished he said, "I'm sorry you were involved in this, my dear, but I think we had better not interfere any further."

She flashed at him, "You certainly aren't going to sit by while Ken English is murdered by your friends. If you do I'll absolutely positively never speak to you again."

He tried to speak soothingly. "You're upset."

"Of course I'm upset. I've been knocked down by ruffians. I appealed to Vance for help and he helped them instead. I want you to find Judge Terry. I want you to see that he frees English."

John Everett's expression grew harried. "My child, this man English is apparently a spy. He took his chances coming out here. If the positions were reversed do you think you could look for help from him?"

"I most certainly absolutely do."

His eyes shadowed. "Mary, by your own account this man was trounced out of the army. He shot a man in a duel, and was accused of being a thief."

"I told you what happened."

"You have only his word for that."

Her head went up proudly. "I'd take his word on that or on anything else."

As if the words came unwillingly from his lips he said, "Has he made love to you?"

She was startled. "Made love . . . ? He most certainly, absolutely has not. That's the most absurd question that's ever been asked me."

John Everett looked hard at his daughter. He knew that he had never understood her, but he thought that at the moment he probably understood her better than she understood herself. He thought of all his plans for her, of Vance Youngman, of his association with Terry, of his hopes for a leading place in the new South.

He saw all these things filtering away, escaping him. He knew that Mary Frances would never marry Vance Youngman, that no matter what else happened, that portion of his dream was gone. His family was never to be allied with the powerful Youngmans of South Carolina.

And he knew that English was responsible for this. He knew as surely as if she had told him that his daughter loved this spy, this killer, this cashiered army officer.

And out of his engrossment with his own affairs he was suddenly able to think of her, to realize what this could mean, and the sadness of it curbed his rising anger and softened his tone, and made him say evenly, "I can't promise anything, but I will try."

"Father," she said, and taking his shoulders kissed him impulsively. She hadn't kissed him with that ardor for a long time, not since she was a child, and for the moment he felt closer to her than he had for years.

"Wait," he said. "Now don't get your hopes high, for there's probably nothing I can do. But first I want your promise to something. I want you to promise that if I succeed in freeing English you will not see him again."

"Father!"

"No, listen to me. There's a lot of trouble coming for all of us. I don't know what's going to happen on Sun Mountain. I don't think anyone knows, but I want your promise, otherwise I won't stir from this house."

Mary Frances opened her mouth to refuse, then she had a vivid remembrance of Ken English, battered and bloody in the grip of Crowford's men.

"I promise," she said in a low voice. "I promise."

John Everett turned and picked up his hat. "All right," he said. "I'll ride to Virginia. I'll see Terry." He moved out into the night, leaving the girl standing stiffly beside his desk.

Chapter Nineteen

The first thing Ken English became conscious of was his hands. They arched terribly. They felt as if all the cords in his forearms had been stretched until they would never recover shape.

He stirred, cramped and stiff and cold. No one had bothered to throw a cover over him. He lay on the floor and he could feel the chill of the outdoors snuffing up through the cracks, heavy with acrid dust.

Only his blanket coat warded off the gnawing cold, and he felt as if circulation had stopped for good. He moved his hands with considerable effort, only to find that in order to move one he had to move both.

He was not fully awake and his sluggish brain took time to realize that he was bound. Someone had looped his wrists together with a tight leather thong. He straightened his legs and found that they too were fastened.

The room was semi-dark although light showed through the narrow window high in the wall beside the door. He wondered what time it was. His head ached dully, but that was almost lost in the thousands of pains which wracked his cramped body.

Lying quietly, he tried to recall what he had told Crowford on the preceding evening. The whole thing lacked sharp clarity. It was blurred, smudged, with pieces missing as if it had been a fretful dream.

He wasn't entirely certain that it was not a dream, but when he looked around he saw the mean room, the dirty skillet on the stove, and then he saw Sam Brown.

It was a shock which drove all the pain, all the uncertainty from his mind. Brown sat beside the stove as if he had been there a long time. He sat, not moving, his eyes watching English with a kind of patient hunger.

He spoke now, across the distance which separated them. "We're all alone, bucko. They rode out before daylight. They left you to me."

English twisted around, using his bound hands against a leg of the table and so managed to sit up. He shook his head, feeling the waves of blood hammering at his temples.

"All alone," said Brown, savoring the words. "Me, I'm going to have fun. I heard once about a critter they skinned alive. I always figured I'd like to try it on a man, if I had the time."

He watched his prisoner's face, and seemed disappointed at the lack of change in English's expression. "You can hear me, can't you?"

"I'm not deaf," English told him. "I can always hear the bray of a jackass."

Brown spat. He reached out, grasped a cup which had been balanced on the edge of the stove and drank with a swilling sound, sucking the coffee through his whiskers.

"A trapped coyote always howls," he observed. "You cut quite a fancy figure for a few days, Mister English, quite a figure. You licked Sam Brown. Know what I'm going to do?" He put his hand inside his shirt and began to scratch his belly. "I'm going to skin you out. I'm going to have me some gloves made out of your tanned hide. And then I'm going to take your head in a sack and ride up to Tom Burke's saloon on Union Street and I'm going to dump it on the bar for all Burke's damn firemen to see. I guess that will show them what kind of a chief I am."

"I guess it won't," said English. His head still ached, but the pain instead of dulling his senses seemed to sharpen his thoughts. "You'll make yourself the laughingstock of Sun Mountain."

Brown dumped the dregs of coffee on the

floor, held the cup a minute, and then hurled it at English's head. "Cheap talk."

"That's right," said Ken. "Cheap talk. Even a squaw can cut off the head of a dead man. Who ever will believe that you killed me yourself? A lot of people saw me beat you the other night. They're going to ask questions. They're going to say it's damn funny no one saw us fight again. They're going to say you either had help or you bushwhacked me. They're going to . . ."

"Shut up." Brown came to his feet in one quick motion, kicking the chair out of his way. His big hand swept up the long-bladed knife. "You're just asking for it, mister. You're acting powerful anxious to die."

"What's dying?" said English. "We all die sometime, Sam. Even you are going to die sometime. I thought you wanted revenge for the beating I gave you."

"I'll get it," Sam Brown grumbled, coming a step closer. "I'll have it, watching you twist while I run the knife into you."

"No you won't" said English. "You'll be all alone here with me dead. You're like an actor, Sam. You've got to have an audience." His voice had grown taunting, and he managed somehow to laugh. "You're being cheated, Sam. You're cheating yourself."

Brown stared at him with red-rimmed, suspicious eyes. "What kind of a trick is this?"

"It's no trick." Ken managed to laugh again. He hoped desperately that Sam Brown's hearing was not too good, that he would not hear the terrible thumping of his heart.

"Just think about it. Sam Brown, the chief, has to wait to knife his man until he has him alone, and tied up to boot. People will always say that you were afraid of me."

"I'm not afraid of nobody."

"No use proving it to me. I'm thinking about the boys on Sun Mountain, the ones that are going to laugh at you."

"Nobody laughs at me," Brown growled, but his eyes wavered about the room. "Maybe I should have finished you while Max Crowford and the boys were still here."

"Maybe you should," said English.

Brown stood uncertainly, fingering his knife. His mind worked so slowly that English could almost see it in operation. He held his breath, knowing that one false word, one wrong sentence could sway the man's hesitating decision. Brown slowly slid the knife back into its place.

"I want to think on this." He was speaking more to himself than to his prisoner. "I want to think on this right smart."

He was silent, considering English, using a thumbnail to scratch his bearded chin. "There ain't no hurry," he decided. "You ain't going to leave right away. I guess I'll go feed the stock first."

He turned to take down a fur-lined coat from the peg on the rough wall, and shrugging into it moved toward the door. Before he stepped outside he turned back, his eyes studying, thoughtful, and made as if he would come back into the room. Then he grinned, and without sound vanished through the doorway, slamming the door behind him.

Ken English hadn't realized that he had been holding his breath. He let it out slowly. His forehead was damp with beaded sweat. He had been so intent on what he was saying that he had forgotten his aching body. His hurts returned now, and with them the dull hammer of his head.

He wet his lips, wondering to himself why he had bothered. He had only increased his mental torture by his talk. Maybe it would have been better to taunt Brown into killing him quickly, to have it over and done. A man died only once, and Brown's grisly game was not a pleasant prospect.

He had no real hope of reprieve, but in him was the fundamental desire to live that makes all things fight for survival, so that when he heard noise outside the door he tried wildly to think of something else to say, some method of diverting Sam Brown's slow mind.

In the moments before the door opened he

formulated and discarded a dozen different attempts, and by the time the strap-iron hinges squealed their protest at being disturbed he had given up, resigned himself to his fate, almost praying that it would come hurriedly.

He closed his eyes to shut out for a minute longer the sight of Brown's gross body, his stringy uncombed beard, his red-rimmed eyes, malevolent as those of a brooding serpent.

Chapter Twenty

It was nearing daylight when John Everett drove up over the divide, along C Street and turned his tired team into the runway of Hawthorne's Livery.

He nodded to the barn man and stepped back to the street, shivering in the predawn wind as he looked uncertainly down the nearly deserted roadway.

It was the only hour of the twenty-four when Virginia settled into a kind of troubled peace. The throngs of revelers were by now abed, the ore wagons that had made their nightly trip would not start again until almost seven. Only the mills worked on, their monotonous stamps crushing the blue ore at a twenty-four-hour clip, pouring the river of silver wealth into whitish bars.

Everett hesitated, then turned toward the nearest of the stone forts with which Terry had set up his watch of the lode.

At the entrance the storekeeper was halted by an armed sentry and paused for conversation with the man, learning that Terry had spent the night in the International.

Turning back then to the hotel's red brick structure, he climbed the stairs and pounded on Terry's door. He was surprised that it opened immediately and that Terry was fully dressed.

"I thought you'd be asleep," he said, stepping into the lighted room, noting that the air was blue with floating layers of tobacco smoke.

Terry's lips twisted wryly. "I never sleep." His big face above the edge of the beard looked gaunt and drawn, and his eyes were circled with fatigue. He shut the door. "Sit down, John. You know Archer and Phelps?"

Everett nodded, recognizing the two men as attorneys associated with Terry in the series of lawsuits which the Golden Circle had been bringing against the mine owners.

Terry lit a fresh cigar and slacked into his chair, letting his big body sag. "I'm bone-weary," he complained. "We've been up all night."

"What's happened?" Everett glanced from one to the other.

A glint of sardonic amusement lighted Terry's eyes for a moment, then was gone. "The fact is, John, that this territory is loaded with venal courts. You bribe a judge, and when you turn your back the other side pays him more.

"Trouble with us is we haven't as much money to work with as the big mines have. We lost our case at Genoa yesterday. And that isn't the worst. Our judge resigned. We're through as far as the courts are concerned. There's nothing left but to fight.

Archer spoke from the far side of the table. "You knew that from the first."

Terry turned to look at him. "Maybe," he said dryly, "but I've an orderly mind, Arch. I'd rather do things with a court behind me than turn this country over to a gang of toughs led by Sam Brown."

They considered his words in silence and Terry glanced at John Everett. "What brings you out so late, or so early, as the case may be? A man who hasn't been in bed loses track of hours."

Everett told him then. He did not know how to explain his errand unless he gave Terry the complete picture, and he had too much respect for the Judge's perception to try to hold anything back.

"I came because my daughter made me," he said steadily. "I pretend no personal interest in

English although I found him pleasant enough during the time that he spent with us. Frankly, I'm sorry I ever saw the man. Obviously he is the spy whom Seward sent here. Obviously he tried to get the men at Fort Churchill to take our guns . . ." His words trailed off and Terry spoke with a trace of impatience.

"What is it you want me to do?"

John Everett had no clear picture himself. He said, slowly, "I want to prevent English's murder if possible."

Terry winced at the word but said evenly, "Go on."

The store owner shrugged. "That's all I promised my daughter, to try and save his life. For myself I'd be glad to have him out of the territory. I'd be glad if I never saw him again."

"You probably won't," Archer said. "Max Crowford isn't the kind to let a spy go free."

"But where are they? Why hasn't anyone seen them?"

Terry shook his head slowly. "I don't know. I wanted Crowford last night. I left word for him to come here. I don't think he's in town."

"Probably took this English to Sam Brown's," Archer suggested. "That would be the natural place. It's closer to Carson, and Crowford and Brown are thick as thieves."

They all looked at each other. John Everett's shoulders sagged tiredly. "Well, I tried. If Brown has his dirty hands on English I guess that's about the end of the story. Have any of you seen Vance Youngman?"

They shook their heads, and he turned toward the door. At the entrance he said, "Think I'll get a room and grab a few hours sleep before I head back. I'm about beat out." He stepped into the hall, closing the door.

Beyond it he heard Archer's laugh. "That girl of Everett's sure took a shine to English. I wish she'd shine up to me."

"Maybe she will," Terry said without apparent interest. "I don't think we'll see that spy again." He was silent for a moment, then said in an irritated tone, "Damn Crowford anyhow. It was bad enough when he brought the toughs into the Circle. It's worse if he starts in on murder himself. He'll turn every decent person on the mountain against us, and the time is coming fast when we could use their help."

John Everett moved slowly down the hall. He was troubled by what he had overheard, troubled by his failure to carry out his daughter's mission. Things had seemed so very simple at first. He was not a fighting man, and he well knew it.

He had a personal distaste for violence, and he had managed through ten troublous years of the gold rush to follow his own business quietly through the various California towns.

It had been natural then for him to take Terry's plans at face value. They had seemed reasonable at first. The whole country was ignored by the east. Southern sentiment had been strong, and Terry had spoken glowingly of how easy it would be to step in and take over, either through the courts or, if war came, by armed force.

But the picture no longer glowed. It smelled of murder, of violence, of death. John Everett got a key from the desk clerk and climbing the stairs again, sought the room, where he threw himself on the bed fully clothed.

He felt as if he had barely closed his eyes when someone was shaking him. He roused to see the lawyer Archer bending over the bed.

"You'd better come," Archer told him. "Crowford's here."

John Everett rolled off the bed, coming unsteadily to his feet, his eyes still sandy with sleep. His hair was mussed and his clothes rumpled, and he had lost the sure, dapper appearance which usually marked him.

"What about English?"

"He left him at Sam Brown's station."

Everett kept his eyes averted from Archer, combing his fingers through his hair in the careful silence, and at last said slowly.

"Then he's dead by now."

"Probably."

Everett rubbed a small, tidy hand across his eyes. "All right." He sounded almost relieved. As he followed Archer along the hall toward Terry's room he thought, I did my best. I kept faith with Mary Frances. He told himself this twice, but for some reason he was not convinced. He had a feeling of failure which he could not quite understand. It had never troubled him before, a feeling of inadequacy, as if at a crucial point in his life he had not risen to the situation.

Crowford and Terry were arguing when Everett and Archer came through the door, and neither wasted more than a single glance on the new arrivals. Terry's face was red above the dark blob of his beard, and he said with unusual vehemence, "Listen, Max. I don't care about this English. He's hardly more than a name to me, but the trouble is that he made himself something of a camp hero by licking Brown. Now he's like to turn into a martyr."

Crowford was having trouble controlling his patience. "You said yourself that we might have to turn him over to Sam Brown. Did you want him free, stirring up everybody about those rifles?"

"No, but . . ."

"There aren't any buts. The time for quibbling is past. Today, tomorrow, the following day we're going to get news that the South's seceded.

Then what? Will the Yankees fight, or will they let us go our way?"

"I think they'll fight."

"So do I. That's why I was interested in questioning English. I wanted to find out what Seward and Lincoln plan to do about this part of the country, and the Pacific coast."

"I think they'll pull the troops out of all the frontier stations. I think they'll have to. In that case, we'll only have Burke and his firemen to worry about, and we'll have all the men we need."

"What about the South?" Terry was staring carefully at Max Crowford. "I think we should be making plans to send men back to help defeat the Yankees in the east."

Crowford waved his big hand. "That's all fine and well. We'll make a trade with them. We'll send Washoe silver to help finance their war."

"Their war?"

"Of course it's their war." Crowford was losing his patience. "We're going to have our hands full here and on the coast, setting up our western republic. Think of it, Judge, with you as president, with me as head of the army." He was voicing his real intent for the first time.

Terry said slowly, harshly, "That was hardly our basic plan. Our hope was to rouse the people of this country against the politicians, to get them to fight for State rights. We can't do that by employing killers like Sam Brown." They stared at each other. "You're kind of taking a lot on yourself, aren't you, Max?"

"Someone has to," said Crowford in his grumbling voice. "You've been so busy fooling around the court at Genoa that a man can never reach you."

"I'm here now," said Terry, and his tone was sharp as a cutting knife.

"Maybe I've done something you don't like?"

"Maybe you have. I don't like people knowing that you stole English from Bowers' party, and I don't like using Sam Brown's cutthroats. And I don't like you giving orders without consulting me, using my name without my consent. It's bad business. Don't think Burke won't make capital of it. A lot of people who are for the South will turn against us when they learn that Brown and his murderers are marching under our flag."

Max Crowford looked about the room as if expecting to find some aid from the other men present. He found none. They were watchful, but not friendly.

He was silent for a full minute, then he said slowly, "I guess the time has come for a showdown, Judge. I'm bringing in Brown's men. As soon as I get word that the southern states have moved I'll take over the mountain, then attack Fort Churchill."

"Attack the Fort? You're crazy, man."

"No," said Crowford. "As long as it was organization you were talking about I listened to you. When it comes to fighting, I give the orders."

"Max!"

"No," said Crowford. "Listen to me." His voice deepened. "You hold a commission from Jeff Davis to take over this territory, to take it out of the Union, to add it to the new confederacy. I want no commission from anyone. I take this in the name of the Western Republic."

Terry's face purpled. "We'll see about that. I've not interfered, Max. I let you bring the toughs in. I let you drill the men. But from now on I'll give the orders. I'm not certain at all that I want you in command."

Max Crowford's smile held a tinge of ice. "You haven't too much to say about it. I'm not trying to split with you, Dave. You can stay with us and we'll make you president of the new republic. You're a smart man, and a lot of people trust you. Together we can rule this western country."

Terry was controlling his fiery temper with obvious difficulty. "What about the South?"

Crowford shrugged. "We'll help them. We'll loan them Washoe silver. We need them. Alone we wouldn't stand a chance for a month against Lincoln. But after the fighting's over I want no part of them."

Terry stared at him for a long, strained moment. Crowford met the look. There was even a tiny smile about his heavy lips.

"I think this is the end," Terry said slowly, and there was real regret in his voice. "We've come a long way together, Max. I thought you saw things my way."

Crowford shook his head. "You're fighting for an ideal, and men who fight for ideals don't often win."

"And what are you fighting for?" Terry asked softly.

"For an empire." Crowford spread his arms wide. "For an empire, Judge. For an empire where a strong man can breathe, can fight, can come into his own."

He closed his big hands slowly as if he already held the western world within his powerful grasp.

Terry murmured, "Max, you're crazy."

Crowford laughed hoarsely. "Why is it that the few men in the world who are sane, who see things clearly, are always called crazy?"

Terry shook his head stiffly. "I'm sorry, Max, but it can't be your way. I've given my word to Jeff Davis and the rest. I think maybe you'd better ride out. There's no place for a man like you in the Circle. I should have seen it before. Some of the men tried to warn me, but I'd known you for a long time."

He was speaking more in sorrow than in anger, but beneath the softness of his words was a steely tone which would brook no argument.

Crowford had no thought of argument. He said flatly, "I was afraid you'd act this way, Dave. I took my precautions. I'm in control. I've placed men who are loyal to me at each of the three forts. We have the rifles. There's nothing much you can do about it. You take my orders or you aren't in on the play."

Terry started angrily, but his searching eyes had already read confirmation in Crowford's expression. "I should kill you," he said savagely. "Traitor."

Crowford's motion in freeing his gun was a single sweep of his big hand. "Don't try it, Davie. The last thing I want to do is to kill you."

No one in the room moved. Crowford had backed a couple of steps so that he had them all before him. "I mean it, Dave," he said as Terry made a convulsive gesture. "I don't want trouble with you. Stay here, take my orders, and I'll make you one of the world's great men."

"No."

"Then you'd better ride out," Crowford said. "Those who aren't with me have to be against me. You wouldn't like that, Davie."

Terry had recovered his natural poise. "No, Max."

"Head south then. You can fight down there for what you believe. The men who fight with me will be fighting for silver." He used his free hand to open the door. A second later he was gone, shutting the door behind him. The men left in the room stared at each other in stunned silence. No one could think of anything to say.

Chapter Twenty-one

Ken English, sitting on the dirty floor of Sam Brown's station, kept his eyes tightly closed as the door swung in. When he opened them he expected to see Brown's heavy figure. Instead he found himself staring upward into the face of a perfect stranger.

It was a question which was the more surprised. The newcomer was a thin man, more than usually tall, and his height was increased by the peak of the knitted cap he wore against the chill wind. He had a canvas coat, with a fleece collar turned up about his ears, and he stood motionless, just inside the door, his narrow, shaven face working as if he were chewing, although there was no bulge of tobacco under either weathered cheek.

His eyes were on English's battered face, his bound wrists and ankles. "Where's Sam?"

To English it seemed from the question that the man must be one of Brown's crew and he said, hurriedly, "I don't know. Some men jumped me, tied me up. How about cutting these thongs?"

The man hesitated and English added, "There's a hundred or more of gold in my pouch. Cut me loose and it's yours."

It was the wrong thing to say. He saw suspicion gather in the man's eyes. "If they jumped you, why'd they leave the gold?"

"Never mind," said English, knowing that any attempt at explanation would serve no purpose, and also knowing that his time before Brown's return was short. "Look for yourself. It's there. It's yours, cut me loose. I'll die for want of water, sitting here."

The man was still suspicious. He snuffed the room, saying half to himself, "Warm in here, fire going. Couldn't have been long."

English heard a sound from outside. It was probably Brown returning. "Dammit," he said, "do you want a man to die?"

The newcomer stirred. Still with the air of suspicious uncertainty he crossed the dirty floor, pulling a knife from his boot top and slicing the thongs which held English's wrists and ankles.

Ken tried to stand and his cramped legs gave

under him. He fought his way back to his feet, using the table as a means of support. His rescuer stood staring at him, still suspicious, his hand on the handle of his gun.

English looked around for a weapon. There was nothing in sight save a short-handled axe leaning against the stove wood box.

He glanced at his rescuer, calculating his chances of reaching the man before the belted gun could be drawn. Even if he succeeded, his arms were so cramped that they would be almost useless.

He said then, "Sam Brown a pretty good friend of yours?"

The man spat, thoughtfully, his eyes on English's blood-caked face. "I've had better."

Something in the tone decided English. He pulled out the leather purse and threw it clinking across the distance that separated them. "There's the money I promised you . . ."

The man caught the purse. English said, "Brown isn't any friend of mine either, and he won't like it, you cutting me loose." He saw fear come up into the stranger's eyes, and the sight reassured him.

"Sam's out with the stock," he added. "He'll be back any minute."

The man threw a quick look over his shoulders. "I'm getting out."

English could hardly walk, but he had no intention of waiting until Sam Brown returned. "Me too."

"Not with me." The man had almost made the door.

Somewhere English found the strength to follow him. He stepped outside in time to see the man untying his horse. Behind it was a pack animal with two heavy packs.

English wasted no time in argument. He made the pack animal before the man could stop him, loosened the straps holding the cumbersome saddle, and dumped the whole thing on the ground.

His rescuer had already mounted. English grabbed the lead rope from his hand and used it to fashion a rude hackamore, then with the help of the horse's scraggly mane he dragged himself onto the scrawny back.

The man, after a muttered curse, had made no effort to stop him but instead spurred his mount out along the rough track which led to the road, and after a second English followed him.

Fortunately the pack horse was a sorry animal, patient and resigned. It made no effort to heave English from its back and he clung there, feeling more dead than alive, kicking the bony flanks in an effort to hasten its lumbering gait.

He had traveled perhaps two hundred yards from the station when a high, wild yell made him turn to see Sam Brown standing beside the open door. The chief was inarticulate with rage. He hauled the heavy gun from his belt and began firing wildly although the range was far too great. Then, as if realizing how futile his efforts were, he dived into the hotel and reappeared with a rifle which had apparently been concealed somewhere within the station.

But by this time English had reached the road and turned into it, welcoming the appearance of a string of lumbering freight wagons.

He glanced back to see Brown drop his rifle and run heavily toward the corral beside the river, as if intending to get a horse and follow.

English increased his pace and as he progressed, the traffic on the road grew thicker. Even Sam Brown, he thought, might hesitate to shoot a man when so many teamsters were in sight, all armed.

As if reassured by the crowded road, the man who had cut English's bonds slacked his pace and waited for him to catch up.

English thought that he was probably concerned about the miserable horse, and the man's first words seemed to confirm this belief.

"There was fifty dollars worth of whiskey in that pack," he complained. He had a high nasal voice which ended on a note of shrillness. "And you put me in the middle, mister. Sam Brown ain't going to take kindly to my helping you."

English looked at him. He knew that he owed

his life to the man, but he could not control a slight feeling of contempt.

"Look," he said. "You've got a gun in your belt. Let me have it and I'll see that Brown doesn't catch you. You can ride on in peace."

The man hesitated. He glanced back along the dusty road, but evidently Sam Brown had decided to postpone his chase, for there was no sight of him.

He probably found the whiskey I dumped, English thought. He's probably salvaging it.

He hoped so. He was so dizzy that he could hardly stay on the horse. He turned, and as he did so it seemed to him that the road came up to meet him, that everything had suddenly spun into blackness.

When he regained consciousness he was lying on a straw tick in the corner of a bare loft room. A blanket had been thrown over him, but he shivered in the blasts of air which struggled through the chinks in the rough shakes.

He lay there a long time, and then he stirred, hearing voices below, and throwing aside the blanket crawled to a half-open trap.

Beneath him was a long room with a dozen men eating at a board table; there was a bar against the rear wall, but the thing that caught English's attention was the fireplace at the far end where three logs blazed brightly.

Painfully he lowered his legs onto the ladder

and came slowly down into the room.

No one paid any attention. The men at the table went on eating. Two half-grown boys carried the plates back and forth between the table and the lean-to kitchen.

English moved stiffly to the fireplace and held his shaking hands out to the warming blaze. A voice behind him said, "Feeling better, Doc?"

He turned then, recognizing his rescuer, and managed a thin smile. "Some. Where are we?"

"My place. About ten miles from Brown's station." A shadow passed across the man's eyes as he mentioned the killer. "You were some beat out. When you fell off Nellie we hoisted you into an empty freight wagon."

"Thanks," said English, and felt a warm surge of gratitude. The man had been afraid of Brown, yet he had not left Ken lying in the road.

"You'd better go back up and lie down. 'Tain't the best room in the world, but I figured you'd be quiet there."

English understood what the man meant. He meant that if Brown came, at least English would be out of sight.

"Get me a gun," he said, "and I'll take care of myself."

The man hesitated, then disappearing into the kitchen returned with an old muzzle-loading single-shot. "It ain't much," he admitted, "but it's the best I got. You want something to eat?"

English did. He ate, hunkered down beside the fireplace, drinking from a scalding cup of coffee which his host brought him. Before he finished, most of the teamsters who had been eating at the big table were through and gone.

When he rose to climb the ladder back to the improvised bed, they had the room to themselves. With one foot on the first rung English looked around.

"I can't thank you enough."

"Forget it," the man was strangely embarrassed, "almost didn't stop at Sam's this morning. He owes me a horse, and I was hoping to catch him in a good mood."

"And now you never will. What did you say your name was?"

The man grinned thinly. "It's funny. I don't know yours either. Mine's Van Sickles. Hank, they call me."

English shook hands, giving his name. Van Sickles' face lighted. "Say, you're the one that licked Sam up in Virginia a while back."

English nodded, by this time accustomed to the fact that the news of that fight seemed to have spread clear across the territory.

"A good job," said Van Sickles. "I'm glad I didn't leave you in the road." He showed no curiosity as to how English had come to be bound in Sam Brown's station. Apparently men asked few questions in western Utah.

He climbed slowly to the trap door and eased himself into the loft. It seemed that he had hardly touched the straw pallet until he was asleep. He slept deeply, without stirring, hearing nothing, until suddenly he was wide-awake, raised on one elbow.

The room was almost fully dark. The window in the gable showed dully, as though the sun was not quite gone outside, but had almost set.

He had no way of knowing what had awakened him, but he listened intently, and after a moment heard a rumbling voice in the room below.

A wave of cold not invoked by the chill air swept over him, for the grumbling voice belonged to Sam Brown.

"I know he's here, Hank. I talked to one of the teamsters that brought him in. Where is he?"

Van Sickles sounded scared. "He ain't here, Sam, and that's a fact. He stole one of my horses and lit out. He took out the lower road towards Clear Creek Crossing. I'd sure admire to get that horse back."

Brown grunted. English eased the blanket from his shoulders and crept toward the trap, the single-shot pistol gripped tightly in his hand.

He reached the trap, opened it slightly, and peered down into the room. Van Sickles was standing beside the kitchen, his long face looking yellow and sallow in the light of the early lamp.

Sam Brown stood across the room from him, big and bulky in his heavy coat. His red whiskers were now tied under his chin and English decided that this was a sign that the killer was on the warpath. He hesitated, resting the heavy barrel of the old pistol on the edge of the trap door, checking the priming.

He would have shot Brown without compunction, as he might have shot a dangerous animal, but he was none too sure of the weapon in his hand. A misfire or a poorly aimed ball would do far more damage than good.

However he held a bead on Brown, ready to shoot should Brown draw on Van Sickles.

Instead Brown said, "Why'd you cut him loose, Hank? Why'd you come into my station and cut him loose?"

"Shucks," said Van Sickles. "He said he was a friend of yours. He said he was guarding the place while you were away, and some teamsters held him up."

"Then why'd you run, and take him with you?"

"Hell," Hank Van Sickles spat. "I didn't take him with me, Sam. He grabbed my gun and forced me out ahead of him. I didn't know until you started to yell that he wasn't like he said."

Sam Brown was not satisfied, but he said grudgingly, "Well, get me some coffee. I'll have a drink, and then maybe I'll kill you instead. I was going to make a pair of gloves out of English's hide, but maybe I'll use a hunk of yours. It's my birthday, Hank, and I ain't killed a man all day."

English could tell from Van Sickles' face that the man was thoroughly scared. He ducked back into the kitchen like a frightened rabbit, and there was a great banging of pots and pans.

Sam Brown peered around the large room, but he made no effort to search for English. After a minute he walked to the rough bar and poured himself a drink. He was raising it to his lips when there was the sudden sound of a running horse outside.

Brown dropped his cup. He hauled the gun from his belt and rushed into the kitchen. English, heedless of noise, ran across to the small window. He was just in time to see Van Sickles heeling his horse out to the road. Another minute, and Brown appeared leading a big gray. He flung himself into the saddle and took out after the fleeing man.

English ran to the trap and half climbed, half dropped down the steep ladder. He ran to the outside door in time to see Brown swing into the trail leading southwest. For a minute he hesitated. Beat out as he was, the sensible thing to do was to get a mount and head the other way, back to Sun Mountain.

But the memory of Van Sickles' fear-ridden face stayed with him as he hurried to the corral, caught up a horse, and saddled it. In the end he turned not north, but south.

Van Sickles had saved his life, and it was because of English that death now rode at the man's heels. It would be well, he thought, to settle with Sam Brown, once and for all. He only wished that he had a better weapon than the single-shot pistol.

Chapter Twenty-two

Ken English spurred his animal in an attempt to catch Brown before the killer came up with Van Sickles, but he had not traveled half a mile before he realized that he had made a bad choice in mounts. The horse was badly wind-broken, inclined to dog, and certainly not a match for Sam Brown's big gray.

The killer was far ahead when the road dipped down, crossing Clear Creek at the old Penrod ranch, and turned into the emigrant road heading toward McMarlins'.

But after a few miles it seemed to English that Brown was in no hurry. He had slowed his gait so that even English's sorry mount was gaining. It looked as if Van Sickles had made good his escape, for there was no sign of the man as darkness began to creep down over the hills.

English reined in his horse. Brown was a good quarter of a mile ahead of him, apparently unaware that he was being followed. He put the big gray into the turn which looped around the flour mill, and suddenly came the distant, deep-throated boom of a shotgun. A minute later Sam Brown's gray appeared in sight, riderless, tearing back along the road toward English.

Ken heeled his horse into a half-run, managing to intercept the gray. He dismounted and tied it to a bush beside the trail, then rode forward slowly, carefully, not knowing what to expect, his hand on the grip of the old pistol.

As he came around the turn he saw that there was a man down in the center of the dusty road, another man standing over him.

A little closer and the failing light showed him that the standing man was Van Sickles, and that Brown lay unmoving on his back.

At the sound of the horse Van Sickles looked around quickly, raising his gun, then let the heavy barrel sag as he recognized English.

"What are you doing here?" His voice was filled with suspicion.

English pointed to the fallen man. "How is he?"

"Dead," said Van Sickles. He said it as one who states something which he does not quite believe. "Deader than a mackerel. He must have thirty slugs in his chest."

English stepped down. Brown had been unlovely in life, but he was even worse in death. The shotgun blast, fired at so close a range that the whole pattern had taken effect, had torn a hole in his chest. His red whiskers were still tied under his chin, but their trailing ends were dyed a deeper color from his blood.

His red-rimmed eyes were open, and they still retained a look of incredulous surprise as if he could not believe that such a thing could happen to a chief.

Van Sickles seemed unable to believe it either. His voice trembled when he spoke to English. "You were following him. I wish I'd known. I'd have felt better."

English looked at the man, seeing the hand which held the gun shake. "It's okay now. He's dead."

"Yeah," said Van Sickles, "dead." And then he started to talk. It was as if he feared to stay silent, as if he found comfort in the babble of his words.

"I was high-tailing it out of the country," he said. "I knowed that Sam wouldn't forget me helping you, that sooner or later he'd use that butcher knife on me." He looked down to where the haft of the knife showed above the edge of Sam Brown's high boot, and shuddered.

"I rode like I never rode before. I took the

short cut and I knowed I'd distance him some, and then I got to thinking. I like this country. I hate to be shoved out of it just because Sam Brown thought he was a chief and was crazy-mean. I stopped at Mac's and borrowed this scattergun. I loaded her with buckshot and then I rode out to the mill and hid behind that stone wall." He was shivering again. "I don't know where I got the nerve." He was a man stripping himself, laying bare his thoughts and not quite understanding them.

"I almost lost my nerve when I seen him coming. He looked so big and powerful on that horse. It didn't seem like a thing in the world could stop him. And then a voice seemed to say in my brain, You're as good as he is, Hank. You're just as big. So I stepped out and drawed the trigger."

Ken English looked down again at the dead man. A few minutes ago Sam Brown had been the Chief of the Washoe. Now he was dead, killed by one of the people he had bullied and frightened into submission. It was something to remember.

Even in the act of killing, Van Sickles had been terribly afraid. His every instinct had been to continue running, but he had turned. He'd stood his ground. English sensed that Van Sickles would never run again.

He bent forward to assure himself that Brown

was indeed dead, and as he did so he saw the butt of his own Navy revolver sticking out of Brown's waistband. He lifted it, checked the cylinder to make certain the loads were still in place, and slipped it under his own belt.

For an instant his hand moved toward Brown's knife, then he withdrew it and straightened. "We'd better move him out of the road."

Together they lifted Brown's ponderous weight, shifting his big body until it no longer occupied the center of the trail.

English turned to the horse he had been riding, and recalled the gray which he had tethered to the bush. "I think I'll take Sam's horse. Tell anyone who asks that I'll leave him at Hawthorne's in Virginia."

"Ain't none likely to ask," said Van Sickles, "but if you meet some of his crew you'll probably be in trouble."

"So will you," English reminded him, "when they hear what's happened."

Van Sickles chewed thoughtfully on his upper lip, then said with a touch of pride which was entirely foreign to the man, "I guess I can take care of them. I guess the man who killed Sam Brown can look after himself."

Together they mounted and rode back to where English had left the gray, then transferring mounts, they continued on together to McMarlins' where Van Sickles halted.

"I got to tell them what happened." He was steeling himself for something which he would rather not have done. "You'd better stop and rest awhile. You're still in poor shape."

English grinned with battered lips. It was such an understatement of fact that he could hardly keep from laughing outright. But he shook his head. "I'll push on into Carson," he said. "There's someone there I want to see."

Chapter Twenty-three

John Everett looked at Terry as the door closed behind the departing Crowford. He saw the judge sink wearily into a chair beside the table and rest his head against a supporting hand.

Archer was livid with anger. He said in a voice which trembled slightly, "You aren't going to let him get away with it, Dave? You should have killed him."

Terry's voice was surprisingly mild. "Killed him? What would that have gained any of us?"

"The insolent brute." Archer took a step toward the door. "If no one else will call him, I will."

"Wait." Some of the iron had come back into Terry's voice. "Don't you lose your head too, Arch. I've got to have someone I can depend on."

Archer turned back, his face softening a little. It was Terry's great strength that he could command a blind loyalty in some of his followers, and Phil Archer was one of these.

"But to let Crowford get away with this, to have him take over the Circle . . ."

"Listen to me," said Terry. "We aren't children. We must face facts. Part of what Crowford says is true. He controls the best fighting men in the organization. Without them we would stand no chance of beating Burke's firemen."

"But . . ."

"And any trouble that Crowford can cause here on Sun Mountain will work to the advantage of the South. Even if he wins. Even if he establishes his western republic, the South will gain because it will weaken the North, will hurt Lincoln and his damn black Republicans."

Archer nodded slowly and Terry went on. "I tried my way. I tried having the new mining companies set up to sue the Ophir, the Mexican, and some of the older mines. But they beat us in court yesterday. I've done all I can here. If I stay it will only split the Golden Circle and make us all easy victims for Tom Burke."

"You don't mean that you're running away?" Archer said incredulously.

Terry came quickly to his feet, the skin above the edge of his beard mottled with harsh color. "If any other man had said that, Phil, I'd have shot him on the spot. I'm not running away. But I am riding back to California. I'll settle my affairs there, and then I'm going down and help Jeff Davis win this war. It's time enough to worry about Max Crowford and his killers after we beat the Yankees."

Archer said quickly, "Then you're convinced that the South will secede?"

Terry gave him a pitying look. He pulled a letter from his pocket. "This came from Jeff Davis yesterday. I got it last night when I returned from Genoa. South Carolina will secede in a day or two if they haven't already done so. Are you going to ride with me, or stay here?"

Archer never hesitated. "I'll ride with you, of course."

"Then pass the word to our closest friends. Tell McMeans that I want to see him before I go. I'll turn the Circle affairs over to him, and Phil, not one word of this outside this room unless you're certain of the men you're talking to." He turned and met John Everett's look.

"Well, John?"

John Everett had been standing there not quite believing his ears. The idea of the Golden Circle without Terry leading it was more than he could comprehend. The idea of Max Crowford and his killers in control of the territory was appalling. This was not as he had envisioned it. He had pictured the Golden Circle as proud men, gentlemen, riding up the mountain, taking over the camp in the name of the New South, bringing law and order where there had been almost none. Bringing State rights, and freedom.

He said slowly, "I . . . I don't know what to say, Judge."

"Will you ride south with us?"

He fumbled then. He saw by the changing expression in their eyes that he had lost their respect, lost the friendship he had hoped for, but he was too honest to try to pretend.

"I'm not a fighter, Judge. I'm a merchant. I have two daughters . . ."

He knew even as he spoke that there were men on both sides of the coming conflict who had far greater businesses than he, far more dependents, who would not hesitate for an instant in answering the call to arms. But he was not one of those.

It was not physical fear which held him back. It went deeper than that. He was a man of peace, who thought of conflicts in the abstract, who had never, even as a boy, had what might be called a fight.

He turned then without a word, leaving the hotel room, knowing as he stepped into the bare hall that this was the end, that he was through with plots and scheming, through with the Circle, through with the glamorous Terry and his followers.

He went along the hall to his own room and lay down, trying to sleep. But sleep would not come. His whole mind was in rebellion. He thought, With Terry gone I want no part of it.

He thought of the stores of powder and ball that had been shipped over the mountains. Some of them were still in the warehouse behind his Carson store. He wondered what he should do with them. Certainly he had no idea of turning them over to Crowford.

At three o'clock he left the hotel and moved down C Street to his bankers. He spent an hour discussing credit arrangements and then moved to the New High Restaurant for dinner.

Finished, he turned toward Hawthorne's Livery. All day he had consciously put away from him the thought of returning home, of having to face Mary Frances, of having to tell her that in all probability Ken English was dead.

On the street he met Tom Burke, surrounded by half a dozen of the Union leader's noisy firemen, and was forced to step from the sidewalk to let them pass.

Yesterday he would have resented this bitterly, but tonight he hardly gave it a passing thought. Without really being conscious of the decision, John Everett had lost all taste for politics of any kind.

He paused beside the door of Hawthorne's office and looked inside. The square room was lantern lit as usual, but there was no sign of the fat man anywhere.

Concluding that Hawthorne must have stepped out for something to eat, John Everett moved back to the stalls which held his team and began to harness them. He had almost finished when a noise behind him made him turn and he found Max Crowford standing in the runway, watching him.

The lantern was behind Crowford, outlining his big body, making him seem larger than he really was. To John Everett he seemed a giant, embodying all the evil of the world, and his tone was not quite steady as he said, "Evening, Crowford."

Max Crowford had a straw in the corner of his mouth. He used it, picking his teeth reflectively as he stared down at the shorter man. "I thought maybe you'd like to know. Terry and a couple of friends pulled out for California a while ago."

John Everett stood perfectly still. He had a bridle in his hand. The soft oiled leather felt cold and slippery in his grasp. He thought, Crowford's watching me. Don't show surprise, don't show anything, don't show the way you feel.

How did he feel? He'd seen a bank cave once, carrying a man with flailing arms into the tumbling stream. He'd seen the man's face, stark desperation stamped on the rigid features.

That was the way he felt, as if the world had dropped out from under him. He'd had his warning. Terry had told him that morning, but he had not quite believed. He had not wanted to believe that the judge would go, that the central authority of their organization would pull out.

But he had been schooled in a hard business, had learned to mask his feelings, and they did not betray him now. He said with an appearance of studied disinterest, "He said he was going this morning."

"Dave's a fool," said Crowford, showing a hint of annoyed bitterness. "He could have stayed here and I'd have made him president of the West. But no, he has to go riding off three thousand miles to fight for an ideal. How come you didn't go with him?" He threw this at Everett suddenly.

But the trader in Everett formed the thought as his words uttered it. "Because I'm no fool."

Crowford grinned suddenly and pitched away his broken straw. "That's what I thought. You know on which side the butter is. I said to myself, John Everett is no man to go riding off for causes. He's a businessman, a dollar-and-cents hound. That's good. That's very good, because we still need you. Just because Terry's gone makes no difference. Some ways it'll be better. Terry was all for law and order, wanted to take the mines through the courts. He bribed the judges, only the other side bribed them more."

Crowford broke off with a chuckle. "The way we do it won't be any more bribery. Couple of days or so we'll get word the southern states have broken free. That's the time we'll move. We'll give the mine owners their choice. They can come in with us or not, the way they like. If they come with us, we'll tax them plenty, if they don't we'll seize the workings in the name of the Western Republic. Either way it don't matter. We'll have the silver."

John Everett wet his lips. "And Burke, what about his firemen?"

Crowford chuckled again. "Can you see them standing up against eighty rifles? They'll run like rabbits. Those who won't run, can't. We'll see to that." He contemplated Everett thoughtfully.

"Had my eye on you for some time, John. You've got a head for figures, and you're good at business. We'll need men like you when we take over. We've got a lot of gun fighters but darn few who can calculate a column of figures."

John Everett looked at Crowford and was surprised, not by the man's offer, since he had entertained some ambitions along this line from the first, but by his reaction now. Had Terry put such a thought into words he would have jumped at the opportunity, but coming from

Crowford, he was beset by hesitation and doubts.

"I'm not much of a fighting man, Max."

"Shucks," said Crowford, "We'll do the fighting, you just set up the business part. Which is why I'm here now. You heading home?"

Everett nodded.

"I'll ride along with you," the man said. "Here, let me finish harnessing that team. You handle that bridle like you were a woman." He took the bridle from the smaller man and stepped past him into the stall. "Reason I'm going to Carson," he said, "is because there's still some powder and ball in your warehouse. I've already started a couple of wagons down there. Might as well get it up here. Who knows, tomorrow may be the day."

He did not wait for Everett's response, but backed the team from the stall and with Everett's help hooked up the traces.

The ride to Carson was one long, continuous nightmare for John Everett. Max Crowford was in a talkative mood. Usually taciturn and a little sullen, he felt a vast and unexpected relief at Terry's departure.

While he had used the judge as a front, recruiting gun fighters and toughs behind Terry's back, Crowford realized now that David Terry's presence had acted as a deterrent to him, that he secretly had resented Terry's popularity with the rank and file of the Circle members.

Terry was gone. Doctor McMeans would undoubtedly try to take his place. In fact Max Crowford had already decided that the doctor offered the best available front for the organization. But McMeans, for all his virtues, was no Judge Terry. Men might accept him as their leader, but they would never accord him the blind loyalty that Terry had evoked.

Riding in the buckboard down the rough street between the long rows of stores, saloons, and gambling houses, Crowford admitted to himself that had Terry chosen to stay on the mountain and fight him for control, the judge might have well split the ranks until neither party was strong enough to cope with Burke.

But Terry was gone. The future opened before Crowford, beckoning him on. The town through which they drove was his, the mines were his, the valley of the Carson was his.

He whipped the team to increased speed as if he was suddenly gripped by the need to hurry, by the need to meet the fortune which was waiting him.

It was Everett who put the fears into words, Everett who said, "What about the army, what about the men at Fort Churchill?"

Crowford was contemptuous. "First place," he said, "They've only got a few dragoons, one company of infantry, and a couple of artillery.

They've got their hands full with the Indians between here and Salt Lake, and as long as Johnston is head of the Army of the Pacific we aren't going to be bothered."

He lapsed into silence and they moved on, skirting the freight wagons, weaving in and out of the line of traffic.

Twice Everett started to break the silence, to tell the big man at his side that he was through, that he wanted no part of the deal, and twice his lips refused to form the words.

After they passed Chinatown, Crowford whipped the horses into a run. "The boys will be wondering what's holding me. They should be in Carson with the wagons by now."

"I'll have to go past home for the keys to the warehouse," John Everett said. At first he thought that he would refuse to turn over the powder and ball, but the more he thought of it the more he realized that he could not afford to. Crowford was not a man to be deterred by such a refusal.

A man who was planning to steal the Comstock mines certainly would not hesitate to break into a warehouse and take a few kegs of powder and pigs of lead.

He was silent as they crossed over the low bridge into Eagle Valley, silent as they entered Carson and turned up the side street. Not until they were within the yard did he see the big gray tethered to the fence beside the barn.

Crowford had already stepped out, and he came around the team before he too discovered the gray, plainly outlined in the sharp moonlight.

He stopped, swearing softly. "That's Sam Brown's horse. What's he doing here?"

A chill shiver of dread rode up through Everett's small body. Sam Brown . . . what was the killer doing in his house? Without a word he turned and headed for the door, his short legs moving like twin pistons in a half-run. He had no gun, but at that instant he could have torn Brown into pieces with his small hands.

Behind him he heard Crowford's heavy steps, but he did not wait for the bigger man. He reached the kitchen and went through it, pulling open the door to the small sitting room and stepping quickly in. Then he stopped.

Ken English was seated in the chair facing the door. It was a question which of the three was the more surprised.

To Crowford, pushing Everett out of his way, it was like facing a ghost.

"English!" The word burst from him. His big body crouched back and his hand moved by instinct toward the stock of his belted gun.

Chapter Twenty-four

Momentarily English was rigid with surprise. He had been talking to the girls and none of them had heard the men arriving. But his natural reaction was faster than conscious thought.

As Max Crowford pushed John Everett out of the way and dropped his big hand toward his gun, English tipped his chair sideways, dropping as he did so and pulling his revolver.

But he could not use it, for Mary Frances, standing to the left of the doorway, jumped on Crowford, grabbing his arm before he could jerk the gun from his belt.

Crowford threw her aside, spinning half around, and before he could turn back English said coolly, "Let it slide, Max."

Crowford let the gun drop from his thick fingers as if they had suddenly turned nerveless. He came about slowly, his dark eyes glittering with repressed hate.

"Sometime, English, we'll meet when you haven't a woman to hide behind."

Ken English rose slowly from his knees. He said softly, "You should thank your stars that there were women here tonight. It would have given me a certain pleasure to kill you."

Crowford lowered his head in brooding watchfulness.

"Where's Brown?"

"Dead," said English.

Crowford's eyes changed. "You killed Brown?" He did not sound as if his mind quite credited the words.

English shook his head. "I didn't kill him, but he's dead. If you're interested you'll find his body at McMarlins."

Crowford was not interested. He had no sentiment regarding Brown. The man had been useful to him, nothing more.

He said grudgingly, "You're lucky, friend. You're very lucky. Are you smart enough to use that luck while you can, and get out of the territory?" Ignoring the gun which English held, and without waiting for an answer, he turned then and tramped out of the kitchen as if daring English to put a bullet into his wide back.

Mary Frances nursed her twisted wrist, sputtering in anger. "You should have shot him. You positively should have shot him. He'll kill you the first chance he gets."

English's voice was mild. "You can't shoot a man in the back."

"Can't you?" said Mary Frances. "That's the trouble with men, they are absolutely, utterly conventional. They have to do everything by rules and methods. I suppose that if you met a rattler in the trail you'd give the snake the first bite."

English laughed suddenly. He shoved the gun back into place and stepping forward picked up Crowford's, offering it to the girl, butt first. "You might still catch him."

Even as he spoke there came the sudden pound of hoofs across the yard outside, dimming as the rider swung into the street and dropped down toward town.

"Too late."

"I suppose," said Mary Frances waspishly, "that you don't think I would have shot him. You shouldn't take any bets on that, Ken English."

"I won't," he said and laid the gun on the table.

John Everett had not said a word since entering the room. He sank tiredly into a chair now, still not speaking, and covered his eyes with his hand.

Mary Frances looked toward him quickly, then said in a milder tone, "What's the matter?"

"Nothing," he said. "Everything. Crowford is probably breaking into my warehouse right now."

The two girls and English stared at him, then at each other. Mary Frances went over to put a hand on his shoulder.

"Something has happened."

"A number of things." Everett had gotten control of himself and looked up, resignation smoothing his neat features. "Terry's gone, for one. Crowford is taking over the Circle."

"Terry gone?" It was English. "Why? Where?"

It occurred to John Everett that he was speaking to an enemy, but somehow it didn't seem to be very important. He told them then what had happened, his voice level, without expression.

He said, "Terry always intended to take over the mines by law. He had his friends file on the ground to the east and west of the lode. He hoped to make those locations stick, but the judge threw them out of court yesterday."

"But to leave . . . ?" It was Mary Frances.

John Everett looked at her and his tired eyes kindled a little. "Dave Terry is a great man. Had he lived five hundred years ago he might have ridden to the Crusades. He believes in the South fervently. He's gone back to fight for it, leaving Crowford and his killers to plunder Sun Mountain."

"I don't think that's very knightly," Mary Frances sniffed. "I'd have thought better of him if he'd stayed here and fought."

John Everett flushed. He had idolized Terry so thoroughly that it was hard for him to hear anything against the judge, and he rallied to his defense.

"Don't you see, by leaving he gives Crowford a free hand. Whatever Crowford accomplishes in the name of the western republic will work to the advantage of the South."

"And if the judge had stayed," the girl said scathingly, "he would have had to condone murder and thievery. So he closes his eyes to it by running."

Everett said, "I can't argue with you. I never could." He sounded almost like an absurd small boy, and Mary Frances relented at once.

"I'm not blaming you for what Terry did, or for what Crowford does."

He waved her away, turning to English. "Tell me, how did you escape? What happened to Brown?"

English told him, and Everett mused half aloud. "Van Sickles. I know him. He buys provisions from my store. I always figured him meek and mild. I guess any man can be pushed too far."

English nodded. Everett said, "I guess I've had my lesson from Van Sickles. I'm still Southern. I still believe in the right of the individual states to decide their own affairs without interference from Washington, but I'm not a fighting man." He turned to look at his daughters.

"You can start packing," he said. "This country isn't for us. Tomorrow you go back to San Francisco. I'll follow you as soon as I can dispose of the store."

"Back to San Francisco?" Both girls sounded shocked, but it was characteristic that it was Mary Frances who said, "I'm not going. I absolutely, positively refuse to go."

Everett stood up. He looked very small facing English, but his back was straight and his small jaw firm.

"I find this very embarrassing," he said. "Once before I offered you money to leave this house. You refused it, and I thought kindly of you for your refusal. Since that time I've heard a number of things about you, and to me none of them are to your credit."

English's battered face colored. Mary Frances said sharply, "Father, if you don't stop I'll never speak to you again. I positively won't."

Everett continued as if he had not heard. "I agreed to ride to Virginia last night in an effort to save your life. That my action served no purpose is beside the point. My daughter promised not to see you again."

English said steadily, "I understand," and picked up his hat.

"Wait." Both the girl and John Everett spoke at the same instant. Then they both stopped, and Everett went on.

"Mary Frances is very young. She doesn't know her own mind. A few short weeks ago she was certain that she loved Vance Youngman. Now, she thinks that she loves you."

"Father!" Mary Frances' cheeks were completely crimson. She shot English an agonized look and then fled from the room.

The door slammed, but neither man looked after her. John Everett went on. "This is a trying time in which we live, and certainly I'm not judging you or your actions, but I ask, as a father, that you let my daughter alone."

Ken English nodded slowly. "I only came to see that she was all right. Crowford knocked her down when I last saw her. I wanted to be assured that she was not seriously hurt."

"We thank you for your interest." John Everett was very formal. "Unless I'm mistaken, Crowford took the gray horse, Sam Brown's horse. I have a rented team in the yard. If you would drive it back to Hawthorne's I'd be obliged."

English nodded again.

"We won't be meeting after this." Everett did not offer his hand. "Nor can I wish you luck with your assignment. Despite Terry's departure, my sympathies are still on the other side."

"I'd think less of you if they weren't," English

told him and turned out through the kitchen door.

He was alert crossing the yard. Crowford had ridden out, but it was possible that the man might have circled back and be lying in wait, hoping to finish the job which Sam Brown had not accomplished.

However, nothing moved in the darkness as he crossed to the rented team and unfastened them. He was just stepping into the buckboard when a sound behind him made him whirl. He saw something white even as his hand fastened on his gun, and he stayed his movement as Ruth Everett came out of the deep shadows.

"Ken, wait."

He waited, puzzled by her action. She said hurriedly, "I . . . you don't take what Father said in there too seriously?"

He was so very tired, and his head still ached dully and he wasn't thinking with sharp clarity. He said, "It's all right, Ruth. I don't blame your father."

"I do," she said. "I saw Mary Frances' face when she dashed out of that room. It isn't like it was with Vance Youngman at all. Father arranged that. Father threw them together. But this, this is different. I've never understood Mary very well, but I know she isn't fickle. And I knew how she felt about you that first night you came to the house. Maybe she didn't know it, but I did."

He watched her solemnly in the darkness. He said slowly, "You're wrong, Ruth. I'm not the right man for her. You heard about the army."

She smiled then. He could see her smile turned up to him. "Do you think a thing like that is important to a woman in love?"

He didn't answer. He could not explain that he knew very little about women. He knew suddenly something which Ruth had known from the first, that he loved Mary Frances. He had loved her from the first time he saw her get on the stage at Placerville. But he had not allowed himself to think of it, nor would he dwell on it now.

He said steadily, "Thank you. Some day I hope that when this trouble is over I can come to San Francisco and see you. Tell Mary that after you leave tomorrow."

"But we aren't going to leave tomorrow."

"You're not going? But your father said . . ."

Ruth chuckled. She hardly recognized herself. It was hard to realize that she, who had always followed, who had always been meek and obedient, was doing this. It was as if someone outside herself was directing her.

"No," she said, "I'll be too sick to travel tomorrow, much too sick. Come and see me, Ken English. Remember, I took care of you when you were ill." She turned then and moved quickly to the house, leaving English to stare after her. He was motionless for a full minute, then he took a deep breath, and stepped up into the buckboard.

Chapter Twenty-five

At nine o'clock the next morning Ken English entered the express company and sought out Dawson, the manager, in the man's private room.

Dawson was a man about fifty, hard-bitten and soured by ten years of express operations in the California gold fields. He nodded as English came in and drew a letter from his desk.

"Came for you yesterday." He studied his visitor carefully. "I heard you were dead."

English sat down. The muscles of his arms were still stiff and his thumbs still felt unnatural and about twice their normal size.

"So I'm dead?"

The man nodded. "That's what they told me. Came in about four-thirty yesterday and asked for your mail. Said they'd been working with you but that you'd been killed down at a station along the river."

"Recognize them?"

Dawson grinned faintly. "Secesh." He spat the word. "Terry's men. They should know better than to try to fool me. I've been doing business with liars for years."

English offered no comment and Dawson went on. "By the looks of your face they weren't so far wrong. What happened?"

"Had a little argument with Crowford and Brown."

The express man leaned forward eagerly. "Say, it wasn't you that killed Brown, was it? I heard Van Sickles put thirty-two shotgun slugs in his chest."

"I didn't count them," English told him. He was impatient to read his letter which he knew came from Seward.

"Funny thing about Terry," Dawson went ahead. "Pulling out the way he did. I guess you know the mine owners are taking over his forts with court orders this morning?"

English straightened with quick interest. "I didn't. Is that true?"

Dawson nodded. "Fact. I saw Blackburn, he's the marshal from Cradlebaugh's court, serving the order on Crowford not an hour ago."

"And Crowford's moving out?"

"That's right. I guess with Terry gone the Golden Circle figures they're whipped. Tom Burke's firemen are swaggering all over town. You'd think from the brags they're making that they ran the Southerners out single-handed."

English rose and moved toward the door. At the entry he paused and asked with seeming carelessness, "You didn't hear what happened to those eighty rifles the Southerners had?"

Dawson shook his head. "I didn't," he admitted. "But without the forts I'd say that Crowford's teeth are drawn. Probably each man carried away his own rifle and that's the end of it."

English was not satisfied, but he did not pursue the argument further. He carried his letter back to the hotel before opening it. When he did so he found that it was not from the Secretary of State but from one of Seward's assistants who wrote:

Mr. Seward has shown your reports to the President who has been greatly impressed. He feels that the Washoe district must be kept loyal at all costs and to that end is sending General Sumner to San Francisco to relieve General Johnston.

However Mr. Seward still holds the belief that there is no real danger that the southern states will actually withdraw from the Union. They have made such threats before which have not been carried out. This department holds that the difficulties can be resolved without bloodshed and therefore I ask that neither you nor Tom Burke take any action which might precipitate trouble on Sun Mountain. We believe that once General Sumner has assumed command of the Pacific Department all danger will be past. Therefore I have been asked to suggest that you return to Washington as soon as possible. . . .

English read the message twice, his anger rising. He thought, The politicians won't learn. They refuse to realize that you can't resolve anything unless you are willing to take a positive stand.

Still angry, English left the hotel and sought the fire house. Not locating Tom Burke there, he moved on to the Union Street saloon which Burke operated.

Burke was there, seated at a small table in the rear room, with half a dozen of his followers. He looked up as English came through the door following one of the bartenders and smiled as he saw the condition of Ken's battered features.

"Looks to me as if you didn't quite get away from Sam Brown in time."

English knew that the story of his escape and of the shooting of Brown was all over the mountain. He pulled out a chair and settled into it, glancing around at the men who shared the room.

"Seems like you're celebrating," he said dryly.

Burke was genial. "Why not? It's not every day that we hear two pieces of good news. First, Brown's dead and that's a blessing any way you think of it. Second, Terry got whipped in court, the secesh were run out of their forts, and Terry quit like a dog. He's in California by now, licking his scratches and thankful to be out of Washoe."

English looked levelly at the man, at the circle of grinning faces. "Meaning you think Terry ran because he got whipped in court?"

Burke was complacent. "Why not? Blackburn moved the secesh out of the forts this morning. Can you give me a better reason for the Judge to run?"

"He didn't run," said English. "Not in the way you mean it. He left to head south and join the Confederate Army."

"I don't care if he went further south than that," the Irishman said, "and landed in hell. It's a good place for him, I'm thinking. Just so he keeps off Sun Mountain I don't care where the devil he winds up."

"I don't either," said English. "I'm just concerned with what happens here."

"What can happen?" Burke grinned at him. "The forts are lost, Terry's gone. Without his leadership the Circle will go to pieces."

Ken leaned across the table toward the fireman. "That's where I can't agree with you. One of Seward's instructions to me was to try and find out who was the real leader of the Southern movement. I fell into the same trap you did. I assumed that it was Terry. I think now we were both wrong.

"Max Crowford is the power behind the whole thing here. He used the judge as a front, but he's the one who organized the fighting men, and he's still here. He hasn't been stopped. He's as dangerous as he ever was, probably more so without Terry to restrain him."

Burke turned this over slowly in his mind. From his expression it was easy to see that he was not much impressed by English's words.

"Crowford is a killer," he said slowly, "but he's no leader, not like Terry."

"I hope you're right."

"Where'd you get all this anyway?"

English hesitated. He saw no need to drag John Everett's name into the discussion. "I got it from a Circle member, one who was present when Terry and Crowford had their showdown. It was a question of who would control the Circle, and Crowford won. He's far more dangerous than Terry. Terry was motivated by an ideal. He was fighting for the right of the individual states to do as they choose.

"Crowford is fighting for power, personal power. He'll stop at nothing to gain his ends.

He'll turn this whole part of the country into a shambles."

"If he can." Tom Burke's tone was mocking. For months he had worried about Terry, and now that the threat of Terry's presence was removed he refused to believe that Crowford offered any real danger.

"They still have those eighty rifles," English reminded him.

"Have they, now?" Some of Burke's good humor disappeared. "Do you know that?"

"I can guess," English said. "Crowford wasn't discouraged because of Terry's leaving, and he sent two wagons to Carson last night for powder and ball stored there. I watched them loading, and I followed them back to Virginia."

For the first time since his entrance the conversation in the smoky room died, and the men grouped around the small tables gave him their full attention.

"You did?" Burke's tone was studied. "And where did they take it?"

"To the first fort, the one just this side of the divide."

Burke relaxed at once. English could see the tension flow out of his big body. "Then that's all right. John Blackburn took over those forts this morning. Some of my boys served him as deputies."

"Did they get the rifles? Did they find the powder and ball?"

Burke swung his eyes over the men in the room. "Which of you was with Blackburn?"

A man at the far side stood up slowly. "I was."

"Well?" There was a tone of grinding impatience in the Irishman's voice. "What about it? Did you get the guns?"

"I didn't see none."

The silence in the room grew. It became so intense that they all jumped as a glass was knocked onto the rough floor.

"Dammit," said Burke, and heaved his big body out of the chair. "I've got to find out about this."

"When you do," said English, "you might let me know, at the hotel." He rose then and walked to the door. Behind him the silence held. No one said anything until after he had gone.

Chapter Twenty-six

John Everett was faced with a problem which he did not know how to handle. Ruth was in bed, to all intents and purposes much too sick to travel.

Had it been Mary Frances, he would have been certain that she was faking in an effort to prevent their return to San Francisco, but although he was suspicious he could hardly bring himself to believe that his older daughter would feign illness to block his orders.

He summoned McMeans, standing by while the doctor examined the patient, and afterwards the two men adjourned to the sitting room, leaving the girls alone. The door had hardly closed when Mary Frances flung herself on the bed at her sister's side and kissed her.

"I positively, absolutely will never forget that you did this for me," she told Ruth. "I absolutely would not have gone back to San Francisco no matter what happened, but your pretending to be sick was a stroke of genius."

"I feel terrible," Ruth told her. "It's the first time in my life that I ever deceived Father, and he's so worried about me. Did you see his face?"

"It will do him good." Mary Frances managed to sound callous. "I could have killed him last night when he was talking to Ken English. I've never been so embarrassed in my life. Imagine having to stand there and have your own father tell a man that you don't know your own mind, that you think you're in love."

"Well, aren't you?"

Mary Frances grinned at her sister. For years there had been a gulf of misunderstanding separating them, but suddenly it was washed away and she felt closer to the older girl than she ever had.

"Of course," she said, "but even I am supposed to have a little maidenly modesty. And you're supposed to let the man make the advances."

"Are you?" said Ruth, and closed her eyes, feeling suddenly a little faint. She wondered if merely by the act of pretending that she was ill she had in actuality made herself sick.

After a moment she rallied and continued. "I've always heard women say that while they let the man make the first move, it was the woman who usually maneuvered the situation. As far as English goes, I don't think he'll ever speak about it unless you speak first. I'll tell you something about him which you may not know. He's afraid of women."

Mary Frances stared at her sister wide-eyed. "Well, I never. You're deeper than I thought. I had no idea that you were even conscious of men, let alone that you troubled to analyze them."

Ruth ignored her. "He's been hurt by a woman. That sutler's daughter who made a fool of his friend scared him. He knows that he can't use his fists on a female, and he doesn't know how else to cope with us. Besides, he feels the disgrace of being drummed out of the army much more than he himself realizes. He'd never in the world ask anyone to share that disgrace."

"Why, that's silly."

Ruth put an arm about the younger girl's shoulders. "Of course it's silly, but men are often silly. I guess you'll just have to propose to him yourself, that is, if you want him."

"I most certainly, absolutely wa . . ." She stopped and on a sudden impulse used a finger to turn her sister's face directly toward her so that she could look into Ruth's eyes.

"Ruthie, I . . . why, I do believe that you're in love with him yourself."

Color flooded up under Ruth's fair skin. "Nonsense." She said it a little too quickly. "I like him, and I feel sorry for him, which is another thing entirely. And even if I were, it wouldn't matter, because it's you he loves. You can see it in his eyes every time you come into a room."

"Well," said Mary Frances. "Well." Her voice for a moment turned shaky, then became practical. "It's up to me to do the proposing then, and you can absolutely bet that I'm not going to let him get away from me. And besides, I think it is simply foul for the army to treat him the way it did. I've a good mind to ride down to Fort Churchill and give Captain Stewart a piece of my mind."

"Mary, be careful."

"Why should I be careful? Who's there to be afraid of?"

"Max Crowford for one," her sister said. "I'm afraid of that man. I think I hate him. He isn't human. He'd sweep anything from his path, anyone."

At that moment her father was saying almost the same thing to Doctor McMeans. "You can't trust Crowford," John Everett said. "I was in the hotel room when he had his showdown with Judge Terry, when he drew his gun on Terry. We all know that they've been friends for years, but I swear that Crowford would have shot the judge, that he will kill anyone who gets in his way."

McMeans nodded slowly. He was a colorless man of middle age, noted for his bursts of temper and his flashes of oratory. Like Terry he held a deep-rooted belief in the fortunes of the South, but unlike Terry, his personal ambition overrode his belief in the justness of the cause.

"Crowford's all right," he said with easy confidence. "He's a braggart and a brawler, but that's the type of man we'll need when trouble comes." A hint of impatience had crept into his voice.

"Terry was a fool, John. He could have stayed here and grown great. Instead he chose to ride back and fight in the East. The country back there is filled with men who will overshadow him. He'll be lucky to get a commission of any kind. Here he could have been the leader."

John Everett studied the man before him, thinking, Why is it that I never before realized how ambitious McMeans is? I'm a good judge of men in business. If I weren't I would not have succeeded as I have, but I never applied the same yardstick to the politicians as I did to the traders. And there's no difference. McMeans is actually glad that Terry's gone. He's learned nothing about Crowford from the experience. He still thinks he can handle the man. It's almost as if he were nurturing a snake. Crowford will use him, and when the time comes cast him aside.

He said by nature of a warning, "I don't trust Crowford. I'm not certain that I want anything further to do with the Circle."

McMeans' fleshy face reddened with rising anger. "Listen, John, it isn't as easy as that. You took an oath when you joined with us. Merely because Dave Terry has gone does not relieve you of the responsibilities of that oath. Don't make us move against you. It's as Crowford says, the time for hesitation is past. The sheep are to be divided from the goats, those who do not stand with us are considered our enemies, and will be so dealt with when the time arrives."

He clapped his black broad-brimmed hat on his dark head and turning, forged toward the door. At the entrance he paused and then came slowly back, having mastered his quick rage.

"I'm sorry. I did not mean to accuse you of being a traitor."

"That I'm not," John Everett's words were stiff.

"Of course not. I'm on edge. It isn't only Terry's defection. The courts have moved against us. Marshal Blackburn seized our forts this morning."

Everett was incredulous. "You mean Crowford let him have the forts?"

McMeans shrugged. "If we'd refused we'd

have had what law there is on the Washoe aligned against us, and Crowford wasn't ready to fight. With Terry gone and Sam Brown dead he needs a day or two to reorganize his men. We marched out in good order."

"And the rifles?"

McMeans gave him a tight-lipped smile. "Don't worry, the rifles are safe. So is the powder and ball that they hauled up from your warehouse last night. We moved it into the three-hundred-foot level of the Gould and Curry mine. The manager is one of us, remember."

He waxed expansive. "It's a perfect setup," he went on. "They aren't working on that level with a regular shift. Crowford is using it to drill his men. They can go on for days without that fool Burke being any the wiser. He thinks he's already won. His firemen are getting drunk to celebrate. They'll be surprised as hell when we suddenly come out of the earth to take over Sun Mountain."

McMeans' enthusiasm was contagious, and John Everett felt himself stirred despite his resolve to have no further part in the Circle.

"But the Fort," he said slowly, "What about Fort Churchill? I know Crowford thinks he can handle them, but he'll find it somewhat different when it comes to fighting soldiers."

McMeans shook his head. "You've got it wrong. We'll wait to strike until word comes that the war has started in the East. At that time we'll take over the mountain. At least half the people in Washoe are Southern in their sympathies. They'll join us once the die is cast. We'll disarm the firemen, hang Tom Burke and maybe your friend English if he hasn't run by that time, solidify our position, and then strike the Fort before Stewart and his officers realize what has happened. Part of their troops are always on patrol, and they'll be highly disorganized with the news of war. If we move fast we'll have them disarmed before they know it."

He turned again toward the door, made pompous and important by his ambition. "Before the month is out, I'll be president of the Western Republic. Stay with us and you can handle the finance of this new country."

He took Everett's continuing silence for agreement, moving out. But John Everett did not stir to follow him to the yard. He waited until the sound of the doctor's team informed him that McMeans had actually gone, then turned back into Ruth's room.

Both girls fell silent as he entered, and he stood for a long moment, examining them, realizing from something in their manner that they were both against him.

He came forward slowly to slack into a chair beside the bed, unaccountably tired, feeling that the end of the world as he knew it had arrived.

"Doctor McMeans can find nothing wrong with you," he told his elder daughter. He saw the quick look which passed between her and the younger girl and his face hardened.

"We've had enough of this nonsense to last us a lifetime. I know why you are pretending to be sick. Your head is filled with romantic notions of not separating Mary Frances from English."

Ruth's cheeks flushed, but her jaw, which usually showed no hint of stubbornness, set. It was the first time that she had defied her father, but there could be no doubt that she was defying him now.

"You forced me to play sick," she told him. "You gave us no choice. You ordered us to leave as you might order one of your clerks to write an invoice. All my life you have ordered me, and I hadn't the courage to stand against you. But I won't see Mary lose her chance at happiness because of your changing whims."

"Whims!" John Everett had never struck one of his children in their lives, but he had the impulse to strike both of them now.

His temper, which he usually held under control, was frayed by his worry and uncertainty and he forgot himself enough to swear.

"Dammit," he said. "Haven't either of you a brain in your heads? This district is liable to turn into a volcano at any moment. There has never been much law in western Utah, but when war comes there will be none. Crowford and McMeans may believe that they can take over the whole district without a real struggle, but I think they're wrong.

"And if they do, will they be able to control the toughs that they've armed? Those men will want to plunder, yes, burn and probably rape the whole countryside. Now do you see why I'm anxious to get you away from here? I want you safe before hell breaks loose."

They stared at him, speechless before his surprising show of temper. It was Mary Frances who found the courage to answer although she sounded unexpectedly meek. "Don't blame her, Father. Ruth was just trying to help me."

He softened then. He was already feeling guilty for letting his temper go. "I'm not blaming anyone, baby." He hadn't called her that in a long time.

"I'm just trying to do the best I can. And the fault is not yours, nor Ruth's. If there is any fault it is mine in believing that I could take part in the Circle, in the plots and schemes that Terry and Crowford and McMeans devised, without dragging you into the mess.

"I've learned my lesson. Crowford is still going ahead. He rescued the rifles from the forts and has them concealed in the Gold and Curry. He still plans to take the mountain and then march against Fort Churchill. If he can win the Fort, he'll control western Utah and then try to rouse the California towns. It's still a breath-taking dream, but I want none of it. I'll close the Carson store and we'll all leave on the stage tomorrow morning. Time enough to come back and pick up the pieces when this is finished."

Mary Frances started to argue, but one look at her father's face changed her mind and she sat, clasping her sister's hand in silence, until after he had left the room.

"He means it," Ruth said. "It won't do you any good for me to play sick now. I think he'd bundle me up, bed and all, and load me on the stage."

Mary Frances knew that her sister was right, and did not answer until she heard her father drive out of the yard, presumably headed for the store; then she rose.

"I'm not going to leave Ken all by himself." She sounded rebellious. "I'm going to drive to Fort Churchill." She was already beginning to change clothes. "I'm going to tell Captain Stewart that those guns are hidden in the mine, and that if he doesn't stop being pigheaded, Max Crowford will take his fort away from him."

Ruth rose quickly, her mouth opening to protest, then she closed it slowly and after a moment said, "I'll help you harness the horses, only, please, be careful that Father doesn't see you before you get out of town."

Chapter Twenty-seven

It lacked a full hour until retreat when Mary Frances Everett turned her light buggy into the main fort gate and drew to a halt beside the guard post.

The trooper, his tawny mustache looking very light against the brown mahogany of his sunburned skin, stepped out, touching his hat smartly at sight of her.

"Captain Stewart," she said, and won him with her quick smile.

"Sorry, ma'am." He relaxed to put a hand on the buggy's wheel. "The captain isn't here."

Mary Frances knew a quick, keen feeling of helplessness. "But he has to be here. I've got to talk with him. I just have to."

"Perhaps the adjutant, ma'am? Lieutenant Crouse?"

She thought swiftly, Crouse won't do. He hates Ken. He's the brother of the man Ken killed. Her voice was desperate. "When will the captain return, tonight, surely?"

"I couldn't say, ma'am." The hint of an Irish smile parted the tight lips beneath the tawny mustache. "The captain doesn't give me his confidence. Perhaps the adjutant will know."

She surrendered then, having no choice, and followed him across the parade to the narrow adobe building. Fred Crouse rose hurriedly as she entered, fastening the collar of his blouse.

"Miss Everett, what a pleasant surprise."

She knew that the boy was flustered, and was not disturbed. Since her seventeenth birthday she had known the effect of her beauty upon men, and had used its power without ever being a true coquette. She was too honest for that, but facing Crouse, seeing the dull color rise in his thin cheeks she thought, If I'm careful I may get some help from this boy. I can defeat my purpose by saying the wrong thing. I'll have to watch what I say, the way I say it.

She smiled as she had at the sentry and saw Crouse's color deepen. "I was afraid you might not remember me."

"Remember you?" Fred Crouse drew a long breath. "Miss Everett, have you any idea what it means to be stationed at a frontier post? Why, that's the first dance either Baker or I have attended for months."

She lowered her eyes, trying frantically to think, to decide what was the best approach. "I came to see Captain Stewart," she said after the pause. "I understand from the soldier at the gate that he is away from the Fort."

Crouse nodded. "That's right. He went out on patrol last night. Some Indians raided one of the pony express stations."

"But he'll be back by tonight?"

Crouse caught the urgency in her tone and hesitated. "I'm not sure. Is there something I might do?"

Mary Frances said eagerly, "There most certainly, absolutely is. There's something which someone must do, and soon or this whole territory will be turned into shambles. Please, Mr. Crouse, you have to listen to me. Do you know what the Golden Circle is?"

Crouse stared at her nonplussed. "Why, I've heard . . . it's a society that Judge Terry . . ."

"Judge Terry's gone," she told him, her words running together in her haste. "He's gone and Max Crowford has taken over the Circle, and they still have those eighty government rifles, and they mean to capture Sun Mountain and then attack you here at the Fort."

Crouse had stiffened and when he spoke his

tone had grown chill. "And may I ask where you secured this information, Miss Everett? Not from . . ." He hesitated over the name. "Not from Ken English?"

Mary Frances lost her caution. "I most certainly did not. I got it from my father, and for your information, Lieutenant, my father was a member of the Golden Circle, and as long as Judge Terry was in the territory he was loyal. But Max Crowford is a killer and he isn't interested in the South or in anything that the South stands for. He's out to steal the mines for his own purposes and he has a gang of cutthroats at his back, and with those rifles he's so powerful that no man will have the nerve to stand against him unless it's Ken English and maybe Tom Burke."

"Miss Everett. I'm afraid you've been led astray by Mr. English and . . ."

"And I haven't been led astray by anyone." Mary Frances was hopping mad. "I think that the army deserves it if they have a war and maybe even lose it, because all of you in uniform are stupid and absolutely, utterly the most pigheaded bunch of men I've ever chanced to see.

"In my own house I've heard Terry and Crowford and McMeans and the rest of the Circle laugh at you, and make brags on what they can do because you all sit down here in this old fort with your heads buried in the sand and prattle about not being able to act without orders.

"And you wouldn't believe Mr. Burke when he warned you, and you insulted Ken English when he came here and tried to make you listen, and . . ."

Crouse said stiffly, "If you knew Mr. English better you'd understand that it's impossible to insult him."

"And that's what you think." The girl was so furious that she forgot all her resolutions about talking carefully to Crouse.

"And you'd better absolutely listen to me because I know Ken English better than you do, and if you had ever stopped to think, you'd know that it is positively absurd to believe that he is guilty of all the things that the army charged him with, and . . ."

She ran out of breath and at the same instant realized that in clearing English in the boy's mind she would have to attack Crouse's dead brother.

The lieutenant was staring at her, his face very pale. He sat down slowly at his desk and looked around, noticing the enlisted clerk who was watching open-mouthed. He had presence enough to say, "Will you step outside please, Keggle."

The clerk rose reluctantly. Not until the door closed did Crouse look back at the girl, then he said in a low, painful voice. "I don't want to discuss Ken English. The court found him guilty and . . ."

Mary Frances hesitated. She realized the boy's anger, but something forced her to come to English's defense even though it meant attacking this boy's dead brother.

"You don't want to discuss it," she said, "but you owe it to yourself to discuss it."

Crouse looked startled. "I owe it to myself . . . but . . ."

"Think a minute," the girl told him. "Think of the things that Ken English was accused of. First he was called a thief. Do you actually believe that the Ken English you knew could turn into a thief?"

Crouse wiped his hand across his eyes. "Apparently he did."

" 'Apparently,' you say, which means that in your own mind you have never been quite certain. If he were the thief you try to believe him, wouldn't he also lie?"

"I suppose so, but . . ."

"But he didn't. He refused to make any statement at the trial. Isn't that true?"

Crouse nodded slightly. "But that proves nothing, both the girl and her father . . ."

"And he was supposed to have done this because he loved the sutler's daughter and she loved him, but doesn't it seem strange to you that if the girl had loved him she would have testified against him at the trial?"

"She did it to save her father."

"Pooh!" said Mary Frances. "You don't know very much about a woman in love, Mr. Crouse. If she had loved Ken English the way she pretended to, wild horses couldn't have made her testify. The truth is she hated him."

"I don't . . ."

"Of course you don't. Now I'll tell you something else. I'm in love with Ken English. I'm not ashamed to admit it. Naturally I don't believe that he's a thief, a liar, or a murderer. And I have some proof. My father does not like English. He offered him five thousand dollars if he would leave the territory. English refused. He came out here at his own expense for Mr. Seward to try and find out exactly what was going on in western Utah, and he would not leave until he finished, even though Max Crowford and Sam Brown tried to kill him. Does that sound like the action of a liar or a thief?"

Crouse was staring at her. "But he killed his best friend. He killed Paul . . . he didn't defend himself at the court-martial."

"Let me tell you what happened," she said. "You won't like it, you probably won't believe me, but you should know before you condemn a man who ruined his whole career in an effort to protect your family. He shot your brother by mistake. He tried to fire over his head."

She went on, repeating to the staring Crouse exactly what English had told her. When she had finished Crouse did not answer. He sat staring at her, through her, as if she were not in the small room.

She watched him for a moment. "But that doesn't matter," she said. "At the moment I'm not here to defend Mr. English. I'm here as a citizen, begging you to take some action about those guns. As for English, don't decide now. Wait until this is over, find that Sutler girl, pretend that you know all about her relations with your brother, that you had letters from him, and then see what she says. Get the full story before you make up your mind."

Crouse rose unsteadily. "I . . . that's an idea. I'll do it. Thank you for telling me." He moved half blindly around her toward the door, then stopped, saying in a different tone, "About those guns. I can do nothing until Captain Stewart returns. That may be tonight or tomorrow. When he does I'll bring it to his attention. I'll try and get action, but at the moment I have definite orders not to meddle in territorial affairs."

He opened the door then and disappeared, and when she stepped outside a minute later he was crossing the parade ground toward the officers' quarters on the rise above.

Mary Frances hesitated, not knowing what to

do, and then, making up her mind, she turned and moved hurriedly toward the gate.

The sun was well down before she reached Chinatown and the point where the road which led up Sun Mountain turned off. She swung the team into the mountain road and whipped the tired animals. Her one thought was to find English, to tell him that Crowford still had the rifles, that they were hidden in the Gould and Curry, that she had been to the Fort with the information, but that the army still refused to take action.

She crossed the divide, her progress slowed by the increasing traffic and she was surprised at the surging crowds which filled the sidewalks.

Beside Carson City, Virginia was a howling metropolis of lighted stores and hurrying people, and C street reminded the girl of Montgomery in San Francisco.

Her first impulse was to drive directly to the International, but after a moment's pause she decided that it would be better if she stopped at Hawthorne's Livery and sent English a note.

She turned her tired team into the barn driveway, seeing Hawthorne's huge bulk inside the lighted office as she passed the open door.

By the time she had stepped from the buggy the fat man had lifted himself from the creaking chair and moved into the runway.

She smiled at him, and under the smile his usual expression of truculence faded and he said with unaccustomed gallantry, "Evening, ma'am."

"I'm John Everett's daughter. My father stables his horses here when he's in town I believe?"

Hawthorne nodded. "I recognized the team, ma'am. Ain't too many like them in the territory. Would you be wanting them unharnessed?"

"I . . . no, just unhitch them, and Mr. Hawthorne, I'd like to send a note to Mr. English at the International Hotel. I don't care to walk along the street."

He nodded again. "A wise idea. Virginia's a good town, but it ain't much of a place for a woman alone, after dark. Will you come into the office?"

She moved past him. The cluttered room smelled of burned oil from the smoky lamp, of harness leather and stale tobacco, and she wrinkled her nose in distaste as she entered.

Hawthorne followed, clearing a place for her at the littered desk, and stood by while she penned a two-line note to English, asking him to meet her at the stable.

Hawthorne took this, folded it twice, and stepped outside in search of a boy to make the delivery. He came back in a few minutes and moved sluggishly toward the rear where he began to unhitch the team.

Mary Frances waited with strained impatience. Outside the barn the constant run of noise from the crowded street filled her with a feeling of helplessness.

What could English do, or anyone do against this lawless town? Others had tried to tame Virginia without success. The place was crawling with cutthroats, with criminals who, fleeing punishment, had found sanctuary on this barren mountain.

And then she remembered Tom Burke and the firemen. They too were lawless in their own way, but they were dedicated to the purpose of holding western Utah firm, of keeping the territory within the Union.

She heard the scuff of boots in the runway entrance and stepped out quickly, expecting English. Instead she found herself staring into the dark, angry eyes of Max Crowford.

For an instant it was as if she had been struck heavily in the chest, as if all the air had been driven out of her body. She gasped.

"Ah," said Crowford. "Miss Everett, all by herself and a long way from home." He stopped, blocking the entrance.

Mary Frances' instinct was to run. She was suddenly very much afraid of this bulky man, but even as the fear came so did anger, and she said, sharply, "Let me past, Max Crowford."

"And let you find English?" his lips twisted in

a humorless smile. "I think not. I don't believe your father would approve."

She stood staring at him, seeing the ready cruelty in his face, hearing him say, "Your father should keep a tighter rein on you, or has your father turned traitor too?"

She did not answer and he went on. "I read your little note. You see, we're keeping a watch on English's room."

"Get out of my way." She tried to brush past, but Crowford put out a thick palm to push her back.

"Don't be in such a hurry. What did you want to see English about?"

She drew herself up to her full height. "That is absolutely none of your business."

"Anything that concerns that spy is very much my business. And you'd better drop the high-and-mighty manner. It won't do you any good."

"Let her alone, Crowford." Tom Burke had stepped into the doorway behind the bulky man and stood there, quiet and unmoving, but something in his manner made the girl catch her breath.

Max Crowford was instantly motionless. His back toward Burke, he held his arms carefully away from his sides, saying in an even, grumbling voice, "Her father's a friend of mine, Tom. I'm just giving her good advice."

"Like you did at Sandy Bowers' party?" Burke's tone was jeering. "At least you haven't knocked her down, yet."

Surprise tightened Crowford's eyes, then he said, "If that's the way it is, I'd better leave."

"You'd better," said Burke. "I've been watching you, Max. I saw you take the note from that boy. I talked to him and found it had been meant for English. That's why I followed you."

"All right," said Crowford. "All right, I'm moving out." He made an about-turn, still carefully holding his big hands away from his body.

Tom Burke moved sideways to let him pass and watched as Crowford stepped out onto the wooden sidewalk and turned up C street. Not until then did Burke glance at Mary Frances.

And in that moment when his eyes were away from Crowford, the man swung, clawing the revolver from his belt as he turned, and sent his first bullet through Tom Burke's head.

Chapter Twenty-eight

For an instant Mary Frances was too paralyzed to move, and in that instant hell broke loose on C Street.

Three of Burke's firemen had been in the crowd and one threw a shot at Crowford, who fired in return, smashing the man's shoulder. Then Crowford turned and ran through the barn, knocking the girl out of his way and disappearing through the rear entrance with the yelling firemen in hot pursuit.

Mary Frances picked herself out of the dirt in time to see Clyde Hawthorne crawling out of the box stall into which the fat man had dived for safety.

Her team, frightened by the shots, had plunged through the rear door and stopped only because they found themselves against an impassable rocky wall as the mountain rose to the level of B Street above.

Already a crowd had gathered about Tom Burke's body, and several men were crying openly as they stared down at the murdered fireman.

Hawthorne dusted the stray wisps of hay from his coarse hair and came slowly forward, saying in an aggrieved voice, "That Crowford, that Max Crowford. He never did have the least bit of sense."

A tall man pressed his way through the crowd, eyeing the livery stable owner angrily. "What's your part in this, Hawthorne?"

The fat man spread his plump hands. "So help me, Peasley, none. None at all."

The tall man stared at him out of cold blue eyes and Hawthorne shivered, then the man turned, and gave brief orders. The crowd lifted Tom Burke and carried him away.

Hawthorne said in a complaining voice, "That Tom Peasley, the way he acts you'd think I shot Tom Burke myself."

The girl had not spoken. She said now in a tone stifled by emotion, "The coward, the absolute, utter coward. He waited until Burke's head was turned." She swayed and thought for a moment that she would be ill, but by an effort recovered herself.

"Who is Peasley?"

"Burke's friend. He's chief engineer of the second fire company. He's a tough man in a fight."

"They'll get Crowford, won't they? I mean he'll be arrested and . . ."

The livery stable owner looked at her. "Who'll arrest him? Burke's men will kill him if they catch up with him alone, but if I know Max Crowford they won't catch him unless he has friends at his back."

Mary Frances looked at him for a long moment, then started slowly toward the door. This time she would not send a note. This time she would seek out Ken English herself.

She pressed her way along the sidewalk toward the hotel, nervously conscious of the groups clustered around the saloon doorways, of their thrown remarks.

But no one tried to stop her. The very density of the street crowds was her protection and she reached the hotel without incident, turning in through the wide doorway to the lobby beyond.

Here was bedlam. Under the heated glow of the half-dozen swinging lamps men shouted at each other, argued loudly about the value of Ophir stock, about politics and about the new wagon road to California.

She tried to ignore them but realized suddenly that she was the only woman in the lobby. The knowledge brought a feeling of panic which hurried her steps and she reached the desk, asking the clerk breathlessly if English was in his room.

"Haven't seen him all evening," the clerk said. "Couldn't tell you where he's to be found." He looked curiously at Mary Frances, a lonesome boy, thinking with silent envy that he would have liked to be in English's boots, to have a pretty girl, obviously a lady, asking for him.

"Is there a message, ma'am?"

Mary Frances had had enough of messages for one night. She shook her head and turning wove her way out through the crowd.

Beyond the entrance she paused, looking a little helplessly up and down the busy street, and then she saw him, almost a block away, coming toward her, his height making him noticeable in the throng. She hurried to meet him with a sudden sweeping sense of relief.

"Ken!"

He stopped in surprise, then reached out to take both her hands. "Mary Frances!"

She was so glad to find him that she almost cried, and knowing this she attempted no words, content to stare at him in wordless silence as the street crowd eddied and pushed around them.

Finally he took her arm and drew her into the semi-privacy of a darkened doorway. "What in the world are you doing here?"

"I had to find you." The words came out of her in little rushes as if she were short of breath. "I didn't want to come to the hotel alone so I stopped at Hawthorne's Livery, and I sent a note to you at the hotel, but Crowford came instead of you, and he was very nasty, and then Tom Burke followed him and told Crowford to leave me alone, and Crowford shot him while Burke's head was turned." She was shaking when she finished and English put an arm about her, drawing her small body close.

"Where's Crowford now?"

"I don't know. It was pretty terrible. He shot Burke and then he ran through the barn with Burke's men chasing him, and I'm afraid he got away. Hawthorne said that the firemen would kill Crowford if they caught him, but that he didn't think they'd find him, and all the time Tom Burke was lying there dead."

She shivered again and he said, "Steady, Mary Frances. It's all right now. Why in the world did you ever come up here by yourself? Is something the matter at home, Ruth worse, or your father . . . ?"

"It's everything," she said, and again the words poured out of her. "Doctor McMeans came and he found that Ruth was just pretending to be sick to keep us from going back to San Francisco, and he told Father, and he also told him that Crowford still has those rifles and that they're hidden in the Gould and Curry, and I thought that something positively had to be done so I drove to Fort Churchill, only Captain

Stewart wasn't there, so I came up here to tell you and . . ." She ran out of breath, and he asked harshly, "Say that again, about the guns."

She repeated what she had said. "It's a perfect place," she said. "They aren't working on that level and the mine manager is a member of the Circle and, and I thought maybe you could get Tom Burke and his . . ." She stopped, remembering suddenly that Tom Burke was dead, that the Irishman would never again lead his red-shirted firemen along the twisting streets of Virginia. "Ken, what are we going to do?"

English's arm tightened about her shoulders. "Easy, Mary Frances. It's not over yet."

She choked. "I still see Burke, lying there. I don't think I can stand much more of this country. It's so cruel, so absolutely ruthless, so utterly unfeeling."

"Steady."

"I'm, I'm all right, only . . ."

"Just don't think about it. Things look bad now, but once the toughs are cleared out, once we have some law and order there will be schools here, and churches and children playing in the streets."

"Not if Max Crowford wins. He'll turn this country into shambles. He's just waiting for the war to start."

English said, gravely, "He doesn't have to wait much longer. It's already begun."

"Begun?"

"The Southerners fired on Fort Sumter in Charleston Harbor on the thirteenth. South Carolina has seceded. A number of other states are preparing to follow. Lincoln will call for volunteers. The East has been at war for some days."

She gasped.

"I've just come from the express office," he continued. "The news hasn't been generally released. It won't be until morning. Dawson promised to hold it until then."

"And as soon as Crowford hears he'll arm his men and . . ."

"Unless I stop him first."

"You could get some of the firemen, attack the mine . . ."

He shook his head slowly. "I doubt that they'd follow me. No one but Burke knew why I am here, and if they would, it would merely start the fight that much earlier." He was half thinking aloud.

"I've one advantage on Crowford. He doesn't know that the war has come. Whatever is done will have to be done tonight."

She said, hopefully, "Stewart may be back at the Fort by now. Surely, with the war started he'd listen. You could ride down there and . . ."

"No time, even if he would listen he couldn't be back here before morning. I've got to do something about those guns tonight."

"You," she said shakily, "will get yourself killed the way Tom Burke got killed and I positively don't want that."

He smiled down at her in the darkness. "I don't care much for the idea myself."

"And you're pigheaded. All men are pigheaded. I know what's in your mind. You're going out and be a hero, and heroes are all very nice, but sometimes it's almost better to be a live coward."

He laughed outright.

"And it's utterly nothing to laugh at." Her voice rose almost to a wail.

"Be quiet," he told her sharply, glancing at the crowd which surged past the doorway only a few feet away. "I want you to promise me one thing."

She softened at once. "Ken," she said. "Why, Ken. I'll promise of course and . . ."

"That you'll get your team and drive back to Carson. No person is going to be very safe on Sun Mountain tomorrow, and I don't want you on my mind."

The girl's eyes had gotten very wide and she was staring up at him, her anger gathering like a dark cloud. Then she pushed herself out of the circle of his arm. "Ken English, you are positively, absolutely the most disappointing person I've ever met."

"Please."

"You asked me to promise, and I naturally thought . . ."

"Mary, listen to me."

"And Ruth warned me that I would have to do the asking and so I am now doing it without any shame whatsoever."

"Listen to me." He sounded harried. "This is not the time and place."

"And why isn't it? Do you know of anything more important than the fact that I love you?"

He groaned. "Look, your father was right about me. I'm not the one for you. I haven't any future and . . ."

"And you are the first man that I ever proposed to who turned me down, flat." She turned away from him and marched out into the crowd, her head high.

He went after her. "Mary, listen. Where are you going?"

"I'm going to the livery stable to get my horses. I know when I'm not wanted."

He trailed her, saying, "Now you're being sensible."

"I'm always sensible. It's the other people in the world who haven't the least little grain of sense, and you don't need to come with me because I am very able to take care of myself."

He came, nevertheless, and he wondered as he put the team to the buggy and helped her in, why he wasn't happy to see her go. Certainly it was the best way. Certainly it would be better if they never saw each other again.

He watched her drive out and down the crowded street toward the divide, then turning he found Hawthorne watching him from the office doorway.

"They didn't catch Crowford," the fat man said without preamble. "The firemen are scouring the streets, but they won't find him, not until he wants to be found."

English examined the livery man with his eyes. His mind was only partly on Hawthorne's words. He was still thinking of the girl and he said, "Why tell me?"

The fat man chewed reflectively on the cud which hardly showed in the natural flabbiness of his heavy cheek. "I run a business, friend," his tone was complaining. "I rent horses to all who ask for them, providing of course that they have gold to pay with, and I keep my own counsel mostly, being a peaceful man."

English was driven by impatience to be moving, but he schooled himself to listen. "Well?"

"There's trouble not far away," said Hawthorne. "I can smell it in the air. I knew it even before Tom Burke was killed tonight, before Terry ran away."

"He didn't run," said English.

"Call it what you will." Hawthorne had never before been so talkative. "A lot of Southerners have used my horses. I just wanted you to know that I didn't seek their business, that I have no politics."

English was seized with a sudden desire to laugh. He understood now. Hawthorne wanted no part of the coming strife. He was trying to declare his neutrality.

"Why tell me?"

Hawthorne's tone grew more earnest. "Friend," he said. "Tom Burke was killed in my doorway tonight. Right now his firemen are busy hunting for Crowford, but pretty soon they'll begin to think, and when they remember they'll probably come hunting me. I'm heavy, friend. I'm too heavy to hang comfortably from any rope, especially since I wished Tom Burke no harm."

"But I say again, why tell me?"

Hawthorne sighed. "Maybe I've made a mistake, but I had it in my mind that you were a friend of Burke's."

"I was," said English, "but I have no more authority over his firemen than you have; I have no authority over anyone."

Hawthorne searched his face with careful eyes, then shrugged. "Thank you, thank you for being honest and telling me. It's time, I think, for me to take a small trip." He turned and moved back into the deeper shadows of the rear barn and began to harness a team with unaccustomed energy.

Chapter Twenty-nine

The Gould and Curry was one of the most profitable mines on the whole lode and as such had already been equipped with a forty-four-horsepower steam engine which ran the hoist and the heavy pumps which controlled the flood of water that poured endlessly into the lower workings.

The Comstock mines had been worked first as surface gold properties, the early ore being crushed in rude arrastras and then washed out in cradles and sluice boxes. But as the mines deepened, as the ore content changed from gold to silver and the veins widened to unheard-of size, the need for better machinery grew.

Some of the mines were more progressive than others. In the Mexican, the peon laborers with baskets strapped to their backs still ran up and down the steep ladders, like so many monkeys, carrying out the broken ore.

All mines had used ladders in their shafts at first and the ladders still remained in the Gould and Curry, although the steam hoist now raised the ore and hauled the working shifts up and down the shaft.

Ken English paused in the darkness outside the shaft house to listen. Above him rose the gaunt structure of the gallows frame. Inside, the big drums with their wrappings of four-inch woven cable almost filled the structure. Below this were the change rooms through which the miners came as they left the mine.

The simplest way into the mine was to use the iron lift, but if Crowford was hiding arms in the underground drifts it stood to reason that the operating crew must be in his pay.

English waited, debating what to do, and as he waited the engineer stepped out to peer around, to light his pipe, and then step off into the darkness. The engine room was deserted for the moment, and quiet as a shadow English slipped around and through the door, reaching the shaft opening and dropping down the vertical ladder to the right of the hoist compartment.

The ladder was nothing but crude crosspieces, spiked to the rough timbers of the shaft, and had been made slippery by the damp hot air and the slimes tracked on them by the heavy miners' boots.

He moved downward as quickly as he dared, his body weight hanging backward into the hot darkness as he fumbled for each new foothold, and before he reached the first level his arms had begun to ache.

As he descended the air grew hotter, foul from lack of proper oxygen, and he was sweating heavily as his feet touched the level of the first station.

A lantern burned, lighting the square room which had been gouged out of the county rock, and he paused, breathing heavily, listening.

A haulage tunnel led away to the left, cutting through a dyke of granite toward the pitching vein. He followed this, stumbling across the iron-capped rails. Before him he could hear men at work, the click of their iron tools against rock, the muffled clang as the broken ore was pitched into the iron cars.

He progressed until he reached the gallery which was being scooped out of the vein and stood for an instant, unseen by the crew which labored at the face, then turning, he made his way back to the shaft and climbed slowly downward toward the next level. Here he found nothing. The haulage tunnel and the gallery beyond were deserted, dark and empty. He used the lantern from the station to search for Crowford's guns and found nothing. By the time he returned to the shaft and continued his way down he was dripping with sweat.

At the three-hundred-foot level the station was quiet, but through the square haulage tunnel he heard a distant shuffling sound which at first he had difficulty identifying.

He stood motionless in the station listening carefully, then loosening the revolver at his belt he checked the loads and crept forward along the drift.

The tunnel was almost twice the length of the one on the first level, for the vein was pitching away from the shaft at a sharp angle as it sank toward the center of the mountain.

It was hot here, and moisture oozed out of the rock crevices seeping across the tunnel floor to the drain which ran out toward the sump at the bottom of the shaft.

As he moved forward along the darkened tunnel the shuffling sound grew louder and light showed well ahead of him. He made toward it, the light growing as he advanced until he reached the end of the tunnel and peered into a gigantic gallery.

Here the vein had widened to some fifty feet, the ore so soft that he could pluck particles of it away with his fingers. The tunnel had been timbered with posts and lintels, but no such timbering would support the arched dome of the chamber into which he stood looking.

Square sets had been employed instead, squared posts, four to six feet in length, mortised and tenoned at the ends and fitted together into a framework which was so tightly built that it seemed like one piece.

This frame, which resembled nothing quite so much as an irregular beehive, its square sections taking the place of the wax cells, filled the entire gallery, reaching from one side of the vein to the other and extending level on level above English's head.

Each level was about six feet above the one below, and had been planked so that the miners, standing on the platforms, could work down the soft ore from the roof, and yet work in comparative safety since the mountain's weight was held by the timbered frame.

The various levels were connected by a series of ladders while ore chutes through the planked floors permitted the blue chloride ore to be dumped down into the waiting cars and then pushed to the hoist in the distant shaft.

It was a masterpiece of engineering, and English caught his breath. Not only impressed by man's ingeniousness, but by the richness of the storehouse which nature had buried in this mountain.

Through the cracks in the bracing the lantern light glinted on the soft ore, on the sides and top of the stope from which glistened streaks and wires of pure silver.

He was not an expert, but he knew that this ore would bring several thousand dollars to the ton and he caught his breath at the enormous size of the treasure trove. This then was a stake worth fighting for, a mass of raw silver large enough to build a city, a state, even a new country.

He understood, as he had not understood before, the force which was pushing Max Crowford forward. With the product from these mines a man could well believe that he could conquer a nation, carve out for himself and his followers a new empire.

And Crowford was here. At the far end of the huge gallery under the light from a dozen flickering lanterns marched row on row of men.

The square posts of the beehive timbering partly obscured English's view, and he looked around for a point of vantage where he might observe without being seen.

A ladder leading to the first timbered platform level above his head caught his attention and he climbed it quickly, any noise which he might have made drowned out by the scuffing of the marching men.

Once on the platform he crept forward carefully. These planks were a good two and a half inches thick and furnished a dusty floor almost as solid as the mountain rock itself.

His progress was slow as he attempted to move without dislodging any dust, lest it betray his presence by sifting down through the cracks between the planks.

He knew that discovery would bring certain death. The men below were engaged in a grim business and Crowford's tone rose hoarsely as he labored to turn his riffraff into an ordered, disciplined force which could stand not only against the Union men on Sun Mountain but also against the army companies from Fort Churchill.

English crept on until he reached a ladder opening from where he could peer down directly upon the marching men, noting with a quick soldier's eye the careful precision with which they answered Crowford's commands.

Crowford stood facing the company, his back toward English, shirt-sleeved against the heat of the mine's foul air, great sweat patches showing at his armpits and across his broad back.

Whatever his faults, Max Crowford was a good drill master and it was amazing how well the men had responded to his training.

Crowford was untiring. It was obvious that the man meant to be ready when the war came, and English wondered how different the scene might have been had Crowford known that already the opening shots had been fired at a distant fort, that the war was a reality.

These men below would form a dangerous nucleus for a rebel army, each trained to lead new recruits. If enough of the pro-Southern sympathizers rallied to Crowford's banner, Washoe would indeed be lost to the Union.

Ken's worried thoughts were interrupted by Crowford's grumbling voice. "Halt, at ease. That's enough for tonight, but I want all of you to listen carefully before you stack your arms. You will have to stay on the alert, no drinking, no leaving town. It's only a matter of days, maybe hours, before we get the news of war."

A cheer welled up through the framework which filled the huge gallery. Crowford waited for it to die, then said, "You all know exactly what to do. As soon as we learn that war has started I want you to gather at the shaft house; don't enter the mine, only three of you will come down after the rifles, the rest stand guard above with your belt guns. Walker, you and Hayes and Dayton are detailed to come after the rifles, load them on the hoist and send them above. Is that understood?"

They nodded and Crowford went on. "The rest of you know your assignments. Those who are to seize the powder houses, move as soon as you have your rifles. Those who are to block the road at Devil's Gate, get down there on the double in case Stewart decides to move up from the Fort.

"Hold him, but don't attack, stay in your positions until I give the word. Whitmore, you have the list of miners who can be classed as Southern. Set up a recruiting office at Newman's saloon. Enroll any on your list, no others. Any other man you meet, disarm him, kill him if he objects."

He paused for a moment, breathing deeply, then said in an almost pleading tone, "This depends on all of us, every one of us. There are over a hundred men here. We have only eighty rifles. That's a small force to take a country with, but because we're organized, because we've drilled carefully, each of you will know exactly what to do while our enemies are milling about, confused and uncertain. Just remember that, and remember that the soldiers at Fort Churchill won't be in much better shape. As long as we keep our heads, as long as we have our rifles, we've a good chance to win. Dismissed."

They trooped over, stacking their arms, and then turned out into the haulage tunnel while a single man, obviously the guard, walked over to Crowford's side.

English's eyes were on the growing pile of rifles. He was so very close to them, and yet so far away. He heard Crowford say to the guard, "You're to stay in the tunnel, this side of the station. The engineer will let no one descend to this level, but if anyone should appear, anyone save myself, shoot them. That's an order."

He turned as the last of the men rid himself of his rifle and moved after him toward the shaft. The guard went slowly about the gallery, blowing out the lanterns, then, taking the last one from its peg, he followed Crowford along the tunnel, leaving English in the hot, stuffy darkness.

Ken lay there for some time, waiting, listening to the distant hum of the rising hoist, then when he was certain that they had all departed he crept to the ladder and lowered himself to the gallery floor.

Here he paused, trying to orient himself in the darkness, and finally dropped to hands and knees and crawled forward until he found the iron-capped rails, then he turned and worked silently along them in the direction of the distant shaft.

The rails curved into the drift and he saw ahead of him the faint light of the lantern in the distant station.

He rose to his feet, and keeping one hand against a wall moved forward more rapidly, traveling a good two thirds of the distance before he made out the bulky figure of the guard between him and the light.

The man was leaning against the tunnel wall, his back to English, the butt of his rifle resting on the stone floor. Ken loosened the heavy revolver from his belt, and crept on.

He did not want to shoot the guard in the back, but if the man heard his approach there was too much at stake to be squeamish. The whole fate of the West might hinge on English's actions this night.

Inch by inch he advanced toward the sentry until less than six feet separated them, then something, perhaps a slight sound, perhaps merely the presence of another being in the tunnel, made the man swing about. He gave a high, startled cry and tried to swing up his rifle, but Ken was on him with the speed of a striking snake, bringing up the revolver and crashing the long barrel down across the man's head.

The guard dropped without further sound, and English stood over him, watching for movement. The man never stirred. Slowly English replaced the revolver in his belt and picking up the lantern in one hand managed to sling the unconscious man over his shoulder.

He carried the guard back to the huge stoped-out gallery, hesitated, looking around for a place of concealment, then hoisted his burden up the ladder and spread the man on the plank flooring of the first level.

Using strips torn from the man's shirt, he bound and gagged him and, satisfied that his prisoner was helpless, he climbed back down the ladder and walked across the gallery to inspect the stacked rifles.

Here before him lay the key to the Golden Circle's power. If he could get them into the hands of the Union firemen there would be no question of Crowford and his followers taking over the territory. But even if he could get past the crew and engineer in the shaft house it was impossible for one man to carry more than a few of the guns.

He might go for help, but a glance at his watch showed that it was already past midnight, and once he left the mine, they would probably have trouble re-entering it.

And at any time, Crowford might hear the news that the war had started and come rushing back to gather the weapons and move against the camp. Whatever was to be done had to be done now and by himself alone.

He looked around, and his questing eyes saw the iron-capped rails which led out toward the shaft. An idea came and he hurried back along the tunnel toward the hoist.

Below the level of the three-hundred-foot station was the sump, a square hole at the root of the shaft into which drained the hot water which seeped continually from the crevices in the rock walls.

From here it was lifted through a four-inch pipe by the heavy pumps above, but the sump was always more than half filled with dark, brackish water.

He stood beside the edge, eyeing the dark water thoughtfully, then turned to where a half-dozen ore cars had been hauled to one side and worked one of these forward until its flanged wheels rested on the rails.

Then he pushed the empty car up the gentle slope of the haulage tunnel and across the gallery to the stack of rifles. Loading twenty into the car he pushed it back to the sump, thankful for the grade which made the work easier.

But he was sweating heavily, and he shucked out of his coat after his second load. The rifles splashed down, disappearing into the dark water, concealed and useless. He paused to breathe deeply, the hot air almost searing his lungs as he turned back for the third load.

The labor in the stifling heat made him a little dizzy and sent a curious buzzing in his ears, but he worked on, ignoring it, and had the car half filled when a sound behind him made him turn.

At the moment he held two rifles by the barrels and he did not release his grip as he came around.

Max Crowford stood not ten feet away from him, hate and measureless rage turning his dark eyes jet-black.

English had an instant of clarifying thought, realizing that the buzzing in his ears had not come from the heat but from the descending hoist, and he cursed his inattention.

Crowford had a gun in his hand, and thus they stood for that full silent instant, all the personal hate riding up between them to mingle with the desperate urgency under which both had labored.

Then English threw the rifles in a swinging motion, one missing Crowford completely, the butt of the second catching his gun hand, knocking it aside as the revolver exploded.

The bullet struck the metal ore car, zinging away to smash into one of the squared posts as Ken English launched himself in a dive, straight at Crowford's throat.

He'd had time for nothing more, knowing that in a second the revolver which Crowford still managed to hold would swing back, long before he could draw his own gun.

They came together heavily, English's elbow knocking the gun from Crowford's grasp, his fingers closing on the man's corded throat, his knee coming up, searching for Crowford's groin.

Crowford tried to step back, his heel catching on the raised rails, and they went down heavily together, English's full weight driving the man's big body hard against the damp, slippery floor.

Ken never had a clear recollection of what followed. There was a nightmarish quality about the struggle, the uncertain light from the smoky lantern, the hot, foul air, the panting curses which dribbled from Crowford's lips.

English fought in grim silence. All the memory of the night at Sam Brown's was in his mind, filling it with a personal hate which blended with his knowledge that he had to win or die.

He had an advantage, for Crowford wore his heavy coat and it hampered his movements, making it harder for him to twist out of English's grasp.

But the man was strong as an ox, ruthless as a lobo wolf. He ignored the punishment he took, making no effort to protect himself, concentrating on crippling his opponent.

As he fell he twisted sidewise, managing to get one boot against the raised rails and use this as a lever to arch his body in an attempt to throw English from him.

Ken rolled as he lost his grip on the throat and coming to his knees managed to drive two short, chopping blows to Crowford's face, then he struggled backwards, feeling for his gun, but in the fall it had slipped from his belt and he saw it on the floor between them.

They both dived for it at once, their heads coming together with a jarring force which sent pain racing clear along English's spine.

But his hand was on the revolver's butt and he kept his hold although he could not lift the gun, because Crowford's whole weight pressed down on the long barrel.

Ken let go, balancing his weight on a hand and knee, and drove his free fist full into Crowford's face. He missed the jaw, connecting high on the cheek with such force that the skin split under his knuckles.

Crowford was hurt, but he held to the gun stubbornly, lifting it, still by the barrel, and clubbed the heavy butt at the side of English's head.

Ken caught the blow on his forearm, thinking for an instant that the bone must have been broken by the splintering crash, but the gun flew from Crowford's fingers, making an arc before it struck one of the posts.

The man went scrambling after it, and English grabbed his boot, twisting it quickly to roll Crowford over onto his back.

The man kicked desperately with his free foot, trying to drive the heel into English's jaw. He missed the chin, but struck Ken's shoulder with such force that he threw him backwards to crack his head against one of the rails.

Stunned, Ken lay for a full second unmoving, and in that time Crowford struggled heavily to his feet and kicked him in the side.

Ken rolled away, sharp pain lacing along his ribs, and came up onto his hands and knees as Crowford fell on him. He felt the man's hamlike hands close around his throat, felt the thumbs bite into the back of his neck, and reaching up, seized an index finger which he bent until the bone broke.

A high yell came out of Crowford, half pain, half blind rage as he let his hold go, pushed backwards and so came again to his feet.

English rolled away, rising in time to see Crowford jumping for the gun.

English's lungs felt as if they had been seared, his whole body ached with fatigue and there was no drive left in his legs, but as Crowford's good hand closed on the gun, English managed to leap forward and as Crowford rose he caught the man under the chin with a quick upthrust of his knee.

Crowford sat down. His eyes were bleary and his hand shook as he raised the gun, but the echoes of his shot shattered the silence of the gallery.

English felt the heavy bullet tear into his shoulder, knocking him half around, and knew that the next shot might kill him.

He flung himself sidewise upon the man, grasping the gun wrist and twisting as Crowford rolled under him. There was another explosion, this time muffled by Crowford's heavy coat.

Crowford slacked suddenly, and English lay for a moment across his body, so near exhaustion that he did not realize what had happened.

Then slowly, painfully, he dragged himself upward, half suspecting a trick. There was none. Max Crowford was dead.

So beat out that it was labor to move, he stood staring down at the man's huddled figure, noting half consciously where the bullet had torn into the man's side. Then slowly he stooped, picked up the gun, and slipped it under his belt.

His shoulder was beginning to pain and he gritted his teeth as he moved back to the ore car and began doggedly to load the rest of the rifles with his good hand.

Somehow he got the car to the station, the rifles into the sump and went back for the last load. He almost didn't make it. His knees were trembling, his head swimming by the time the last rifle slipped from sight beneath the surface of the dark water.

He sat down, too exhausted to move. His shirt and the shoulder of his coat were sticky with drying blood. He sat there a long time, but finally dragged himself to his feet and half walked, half staggered to the hoist.

He knew he had to get out of there, that if Crowford's men found him in the mine it would be the end. Carefully he climbed aboard the iron basket and signaled the engineer to hoist him up.

The man's face when English stepped from the lift was a study in startled consternation. He stared at Ken as if English had been a ghost, at the gun which Ken held level as if he had never seen a revolver before.

"Where's Crowford?"

"Dead," said English, knowing that the engineer would immediately get in touch with the Circle members. But it was already gray daylight outside the shaft house, it would be only a little while before the news that the war had started would be all over the mountain.

"There's a man down there," he added, "bound and gagged. You'd better release him before he smothers." Then, still carrying the gun in his hand, he turned out of the mine building and headed slowly toward the hotel.

Chapter Thirty

Sun Mountain came awake with a start to find that the country was at war. Bulletins outside the newspaper office carried the account of the attack on Fort Sumter, and those of the Circle who had not already heard of Crowford's death raced to the Gould and Curry.

Doctor McMeans was there, trying to bring some order out of chaos. They had searched the workings thoroughly, never once thinking to fish in the black waters of the sump, and now had moved up the hill to Johnny Newman's saloon. Above the building, whipping in the morning breeze, flew a new flag, crossed bars and stars, the secession flag.

Despite the house doctor's protest English re-fused to remain at the hotel. He stepped out into the early morning sunlight and joined the growing crowd which had gathered across the street from Newman's, watching the Southerners who stood in a tight knot to the right of the building entrance.

Johnny Newman, a shotgun on his shoulder, paraded back and forth before the open saloon door as if daring anyone to cross the street and attempt to tear down the Southern flag.

The situation was tense and growing more explosive by the minute. The Circle men, without Crowford, and without the rifles, were confused. All their carefully planned moves were stalemated by the lack of weapons, and they waited around McMeans while the doctor tried to decide what to do.

The firemen were gathered across the street, keeping a little separate from the huge crowd of ordinary citizens who stood bewilderedly leaderless, not quite understanding what had happened.

Without Burke, Tom Peasley was in control and from his angry face, and the sullen expression of his men, it was easy to see that they were as disordered as were their Southern opponents.

As Ken English came slowly up the hill to join the crowd he heard Peasley say in a tight, high voice, "Waterman, go get a flag, a real flag, and plant it high on Newman's roof."

One of the firemen turned and raced past English, down the steep street toward C. He was back in less than five minutes, carrying a flag. He never hesitated, but pushed through the crowd and crossed the empty street.

There were angry growls from the Southerners. Johnny Newman swung the shotgun from his shoulder and held it at ready. Peasley's voice came even and steady above the sudden silence which blanketed the waiting crowd. "I'll shoot the first man that bothers you, keep going." You could hear the click as he pulled back the hammer on his big revolver.

Waterman had never hesitated. He made directly for the corner of the building. No one moved in the street. No sound came. The firemen waited with drawn guns. The Southerners faced them, angry, sullen.

Johnny Newman lifted his shotgun to his shoulder, sighting along it at the flag, but before he could pull the trigger and change the street into a battleground, the high, sharp sound of a bugle cut above the cheers and a company of dragoons swept up C Street, turned, cutting up the hill to B, and drove between the embattled groups.

Lieutenant Baker rode his horse up onto the sidewalk, staring down at the startled Newman. "Who put up that flag?" He pointed with his bared saber at the Southern colors.

Newman flushed, his angry eyes running

along the even line of mounted men. Silently he dropped his shotgun and turning, mounted to the roof where he pulled down the secession flag.

English had pushed through the crowd and stepping between the mounted men, looked up at Baker. The lieutenant acknowledged his presence with a slight nod. "There are eighty rifles, government property in this camp. Where are they, Mr. English?" His eyes were on Ken's battered face, his bandaged shoulder.

"At the bottom of the Gould and Curry sump, Lieutenant."

Baker's eyes flickered with surprise. "I've orders to arrest a man named Crowford," his attention went to the grouped Circle men. "Where is he?"

"Dead," said English. "His body is also in the Gould and Curry."

Baker had turned back, his eyes noting the extent of English's hurts, his quick mind drawing its own conclusion. "It seems that we arrived too late."

English looked at the sullen Southerners, at the jubilant firemen, and he shook his head. "No," he told Baker softly. "I think you got here just in time. Two minutes more and you'd have ridden into a battle royal. Frankly, I'm both surprised and pleased to see you."

Baker tugged thoughtfully at one corner of his

straw-colored mustache. "Thank Miss Everett. She came driving in the middle of the night and raised the whole fort."

The sun wrinkles at the corners of his eyes crinkled. "I'll wager that no war department official ever ate-out a captain the way she jumped on poor Jasper Stewart. She's quite a girl."

English was staring at him, nonplussed.

"She's on her way up here," Baker added as if in after-thought. "Her team was pretty well beat out and couldn't keep up with us, but unless I miss my guess she'll be along in a few minutes."

He turned back then, drawing a piece of paper from his pouch. "Sergeant, dismount ten men. Arrest these men." He handed the paper to Mike Lynch who swung down from his horse, and then certain that Baker's eyes were no longer on him, forgot himself enough to wink at English. He held up the paper, reading the names.

"Max Crowford, dead. Captain Hall. Doctor McMeans . . ."

English turned away. Baker said, "We'll take their leaders down to the Fort and let them fill sandbags for a few days; that should give them a bellyful of war."

Ken nodded absently and walked slowly down the hill to C Street. As he came opposite Hawthorne's livery he saw a light team appear over the divide and guessed that it was the girl. He stood there, waiting for her to drive up, conscious of a quickening excitement and thought, This won't do, this won't do at all, and then as the light buggy swept forward he realized that she was not alone, and stiffened as he recognized Fred Crouse at the reins.

He turned quickly about and started to walk away, but her sharp call stopped him. "Ken, Ken English. You come here."

He stopped, turned slowly and walked back to where Crouse had turned the buggy into the livery entrance.

The girl's eyes shadowed with quick concern as she noted the bruises on his face, the bandaged shoulder, and her voice was not quite steady as she said, "Well, anyhow, you're still alive. It's almost more than I dared hope." And then her face broke as the tears of relief came and she was out of the buggy with both arms around his neck. "Ken. You're all right?"

He steadied her with his good hand. "I'm fine, and your soldiers got here just in time." He looked across her head at the silent Crouse and said in a tight voice, "Thank you for driving her up, Lieutenant."

"Ken," said the girl. "You listen to me. I told him all about it yesterday afternoon, all the things you should have told him yourself and didn't. . . ."

"And I," said Crouse, clearing his throat somewhat noisily, "took the liberty of writing to

Washington last night, asking that the matter be reopened. I think, with the war and . . ."

He broke off, not finding the proper words, and the girl said, "So now you haven't got any excuse for not marrying me, and you might have the decency not to make me do all the asking and . . ."

He smiled down at her in spite of himself, then looked up into Crouse's eyes, saying, simply, "Thanks, Fred, I . . ."

Crouse waited for no more. He shook the reins, driving on into the barn. English looked down into the girl's face. He said slowly, "Listen to me, Mary. The war is here, and I'll be in it, somehow, whether I'm reinstated or not. Afterwards, when this mess is settled, will be time enough for . . ."

"Oh, no you don't. You absolutely don't. The war may last for years, and you'll get a chance to meet a lot of girls, and I'm positively not going to take the chance. You're going to marry me before you ever get out of western Utah. Haven't you learned by now that once I make up my mind, I always have my way?"

He didn't argue further. Instead he bent and kissed her. "Is that better?"

"That," said Mary Frances when she had recovered her breath, "is absolutely, utterly perfect. I couldn't have done a better job myself. I really truly couldn't. Try it again."

Todhunter Ballard was born in Cleveland, Ohio. He graduated with a bachelor's degree from Wilmington College in Ohio, having majored in mechanical engineering. His early years were spent working as an engineer before he began writing fiction for the magazine market. As W.T. Ballard, he was one of the regular contributors to *Black Mask Magazine*, along with Dashiell Hammett and Erle Stanley Gardner. Although Ballard published his first Western story in *Cowboy Stories* in 1936, the same year he married Phoebe Dwiggins, it wasn't until *Two-Edged Vengeance* (1951) that he produced his first Western novel. Ballard later claimed that Phoebe, following their marriage, had cowritten most of his fiction with him and perhaps this explains, in part, his memorable female characters. Ballard's golden age as a Western author came in the 1950s and extended to the early 1970s. *Incident At Sun Mountain* (1952), *West Of Quarantine* (1953), and *High Iron* (1953) are among his finest early historical titles. After numerous traditional Westerns for various publishers, Ballard returned to the historical novel in *Gold In California!* (1965), which earned him a Golden Spur Award from the Western Writers of America. This story is set during the Gold Rush era of the 'Forty-Niners. However, an even more panoramic view of that same era is to be found in Ballard's magnum opus, *The Californian* (1971), which contrasts the *Californios* and the emigrant goldseekers while detailing the building of a freight line to compete with Wells Fargo. In his historical fiction, Ballard combined his background in engineering with exhaustive historical research. These novels are character driven, gripping a reader from first page to last with their inherent drama and the spirit of adventure so true of those times.